Scent of a $windle

(A Josephine Stuart Mystery)

by

Joyce Oroz

Copyright 2015 by Joyce Oroz

For information, email **Cozy Cat Press**, cozycatpress@aol.com or visit our website at: www.cozycatpress.com

COZY CAT PRESS

ISBN: 978-1-939816-75-7

Printed in the United States of America

Cover by Paula Ellenberger
http://www.paulaellenberger.com/ design

1 2 3 4 5 6 7 8 9 10

I am dedicating this book to my wonderful husband, author, Arthur C. Oroz , because he inspired me to write. He had no idea at the time that I would not be able to stop. Thank you, dear, for putting up with my many hours at the computer.

Dear friends, I love telling stories. What could be more fun? But without my wonderful support group there would be no books. Tomi Edmiston corrects my work and puts it into the proper form. Thank you, Tomi, for your hard work and kind heart. As always, thank you to my husband, Art, for his good advice and common sense. Thank you, Patricia Rockwell, owner and founder of Cozy Cat Press. It is a real pleasure working with you!

Chapter One

Barely awake Sunday morning, September fifth, I stumbled down an unfamiliar hallway, moving toward glints of moonlight from a bank of kitchen windows. Why was my cell phone ringing at three a.m.? "Should have left it by the bed," I grumbled to Solow. Images of emergencies, disasters and my elderly parents shot through sleep-deprived brain cells. I found my purse hooked on a chair and frantically fumbled through the clutter inside, tossing aside tissues, receipts, gum wrappers, a checkbook, a half-eaten power bar and some loose change.

Solow put his nose to the back door and barked.

"Not now, I have to answer…oh darn it; it's going to be a message." I put the cell phone down, let my basset out the back door and thought I found a light switch, but it turned out to be a garbage disposal that jarred the bananas out of me. As I stood by the door waiting for Solow to reappear, my hand found the real light switch.

"What in Sam Hill?" a voice screamed.

"Quiet, bird!" I snapped at the large cockatoo perched on a dowel stretching across his three-foot by three-foot by six-foot tall wire cage, wedged between a loaded china cabinet on the left and a fearful portrait of Tom Trippy's grandmother on the right. Solow and I were in the Trippys' home at three in the morning because I had agreed to babysit their house and a newly-acquired cockatoo named Boris, better known as Bad Boy.

"Sorry, Boris, calm down, and don't screech at me!" Clutching the phone in one hand, I pushed the light switch down. Instantly, quiet darkness returned. I let Solow back into the kitchen and felt my way along the hall to my assigned room, a three-hundred-square-foot guest bedroom featuring rosewood furniture with fancy silk, lace and ruffled accessories. Fancy had no place in my "normal" life as a country girl artist.

White carpet prevailed in the four-thousand-square-foot, single-story house on top of a knoll in Prunedale, California. Tom and Lois Trippy had planned a thirty-day trip to Europe long before they'd unexpectedly inherited Boris from their neighbor at the bottom of the hill. Their neighbor, ninety-seven-year-old Henry Hobblestone had died from an accidental gunshot wound, the local newspaper reported. "The elderly man was obviously cleaning his rifle when it accidentally went off."

Henry had promised to give Lois his bird when he died. Or maybe he made Lois promise to take the bird *if* he died. Either way, Lois was tied to the care of an eighteen-year-old snowy white cockatoo with peach-colored cheeks and under-wings. After forty years of a childless marriage with no pets and plenty of white carpet, the Trippy life style would certainly change now that Boris had arrived.

Saturday, September 4th, Boris and his cage arrived at the Trippy house—the same day Lois and Tom left for Europe, and the same day I arrived as temporary caretaker. The couple apologized as they loaded suitcases into the car, hardly noticing two men and a bird entering the house. After a few last minute instructions for me, the Trippys drove away, focused on the San Jose Airport and their flight to Europe.

Boris rode on Marvin's shoulder while Marvin's brother, Allen, angled a rusty ramp against the tailgate of their faded red Chevy pickup truck decked out in patches of gray primer. Allen rolled a large wire cage down the ramp, through the four-car garage, and into the Trippys' spacious kitchen. It clanked across the tile floor, coming to a stop against the west wall.

Marvin leaned into the cage, pushed the big cockatoo off his shoulder onto a perch, withdrew his lanky body and closed the wire door.

"Boris wants a cracker," the bird squawked as the door closed.

I laughed. "That's so cute! I love the way his head feathers shoot up when he's emotional. His feathers are so white and pretty, and I love those peachy pink cheeks."

"I'll be back in a minute," Allen uttered without making eye contact.

He came back from his truck with newspapers and water and food dispensers for the cage. When everything was in place, the middle-aged brothers hung around looking like they expected something. Finally, Marvin asked if Mrs. Trippy had left a check for them.

"Not that I'm aware of," I said, scanning the instruction list Lois had left on the counter. "How much were you expecting?"

"A hundred dollars, ma'am."

"I'm sorry but the Trippys won't be back for a month."

"Ain't easy being a handyman," Allen grumped, his lower lip sucked in behind a droopy mustache, blue eyes trained on a floor tile.

"Sometimes we never see the money," Marvin chimed in. "Handyman stuff ain't easy, that's why folks call us...."

"Okay, don't worry; I'll write you a check." I found my checkbook in my purse. "Who do I write this to?"

"Ace Handyman Brothers, and thank you, ma'am."

"No problem." The Trippys had left me a check for five hundred dollars for house sitting. I wasn't in it for the money, but I didn't refuse it either. My career as a mural painter paid well enough, but as a widow I had one unsteady income, a mortgage to pay and a dog to feed.

Saturday morning, I had packed my clothes and Solow's bed and kibble and left my home in Aromas. I drove twelve miles south to the Trippys' house in Prunedale, a small town sliced in half by Highway 101.

My hometown Aromas was ten times smaller than Prunedale. It had one three-way stop, a handful of businesses including a post office, a school and a church. Just a half mile from downtown Aromas, my little adobe house sat on five hilly acres surrounded by more hills, grass and spreading oaks. Ocean breezes and wispy fog frequently blew ten miles inland to ventilate and invigorate my neighbors and me.

Now I sat in the dark on Lois Trippy's snow-white duvet, checking my phone. I didn't recognize the number, but pushed the send button anyway. Whoever had awakened me at three in the morning was about to get a piece of my mind.

"Josephine, thank you for calling."

"Lois, is that you?" I waited several seconds.

"That's right, dear, is everything okay? You sound funny," she giggled.

"I'm fine, Lois, but it's three-thirty in the morn...."

"Oh, dear. I'm so sorry, Josephine. You see, it's almost noon here. It's lovely in Paris and I wanted to share....oh well, another time. Get a good night's sleep, dear." She hung up.

I crawled under the covers and closed my eyes, teeth still clenched. How did I get myself into this? Actually, I was doing a favor for David Galaz, my neighbor and very close friend. He could not fulfill his promise to house sit for the Trippys because his beautiful but temperamental cat, Ms. Fluffy, unexpectedly had had four kittens even though the veterinarian had been paid years ago to make sure that that sort of thing didn't happen. At the last minute, David had to find a substitute house sitter, so he asked me.

Before their retirement, Mr. Trippy had been David's boss at IBM in San Jose, a big man in a big industry. Lois didn't have a career and was several years younger than Tom.

Recently retired, David lived on his five acres next door to me in Aromas. I planned to visit him when I found time between my new mural job at the Crazy Horse Saloon in San Juan Bautista, and taking care of the Trippy homestead in Prunedale. On a map, Aromas, Prunedale and San Juan Bautista formed a forty-five-mile triangle, roughly fifteen miles between each town. I was resigned to spending lots of time driving the *triangle* in my aging red Mazda pickup truck.

I snatched a bit of sleep before the sun came up and the Big Bird alarm went off in the kitchen. It sounded like Boris said, "Where's wawa? Where's wawa?" It was five-thirty in the morning. I hoped Boris would run out of things to say and let me sleep, but the chatter continued, something about Henry and five more minutes. I put the pillow over my head, but all that did was muffle the bird's chatter into a noisy cacophony.

Solow snored in his bed across the room from me, loving a good sleepover, anywhere, anytime.

I tossed and turned until six o'clock, a more decent time to get out of bed, shower and look after Boris. When I did, it looked like he hadn't touched his food and water. He eyed my pink plaid shirt with one red eyeball.

"Boris wants a cracker."

"Boris can wait until I have my coffee."

"Boris wants a cracker."

"Stuff it, Boris." I found a coffeemaker and filters, but where were the coffee beans? I checked all nine thousand cupboards and drawers and found not one stitch of food or drink. Finally, I opened a door, turned on the light and discovered shelves of canned foods, cereals, crackers, pastas and a sack of Peet's ground coffee. I couldn't think of anything better than Sunday morning with a good cup of coffee and a newspaper, unless it was a visit with David.

I shuffled through the house and out the front door. The air felt cool and crisp. Solow trotted outside to be with me and stayed by my side as I searched for a newspaper in the dim light of a pinkish sunrise.

Suddenly, I straightened up and turned toward the roar of a tripped-out silver Honda sedan charging up the driveway. A rolled-up newspaper flew past my right ear, smashing into a potted pelargonium positioned a couple of feet from the over-sized mahogany front doors. The car never slowed, just squealed around the circle drive and swished down the hill like a winter gully washer.

Solow sniffed the concrete and followed his nose to a rose garden infiltrated by concrete gnomes. The little guys in pointy red hats had Solow surrounded. He looked back at me, tucked in his tail and galloped to my side.

Back to the warm kitchen and a mug of coffee, I opened the paper and sorted want-to-read pages from don't-give-a-hoot pages. A name in the obits caught my eye: Henry Hobblestone, the Trippys' deceased, ninety-seven-year-old neighbor. According to the article, Henry had never married. He was survived by a niece who lived in Texas. Henry looked about seventy years old in the old grainy black and white photo. Seriously somber, with fine features and thick white hair, he stared at the camera as if it were a gun.

Following the traditional article about Henry's death, was another article from the coroner who stated that *Henry* was discovered to be a woman. She had worn men's clothing, had short hair and wore no makeup. Her identification said she was a man named Henry Hobblestone.

My mouth dropped open. How could...why would someone pretend to be the opposite sex? How long had she fooled everyone?

Ironically, Henry had died from a gunshot wound while cleaning his/her rifle. Although Henry had been known to be a good shot, Lois told me that he routinely chased and shot at wild turkeys but had never even winged one in the last twenty years. Wild turkeys invaded properties all over Monterey County, looking for an easy meal. By law, they were protected. If anyone thought these turkeys would make an easy Thanksgiving dinner, they were delusional. The tough old birds were fast and smart, unlike their caged cousins that didn't know a gun from a toothpick.

Did Lois know he was a she? I wondered. *Did anyone know?*

When I finished reading the obituaries, I tore the Henry article out of the paper, leaned ninety percent of my fifty-year-old full-figured body into Boris' cage and spread the rest of the paper over the first layer of newspaper.

Boris craned his neck; one dark beady eye followed my activity.

"Boris wants a cracker."

"Boris doesn't need a cracker, be quiet and read the paper."

"Back up, now!"

"What?"

"Back up, now!" he repeated.

I backed out of the cage and closed the door.

"Stuff it, Boris. You're an aggressive old bird, aren't you?"

"Hands up!" he demanded, as he fluffed and pointed his feathers toward the ceiling.

"I think you've been watching too many cowboy movies."

"Stuff it, Boris, stuff it, Boris," he said, cocking his snowy head to one side, his beak not quite shut. *Do birds like to bite people?* I wondered. Boris twisted his neck backward and began preening his lovely white feathers, ignoring me completely.

Solow had whined and worried the whole time I was inside the cage. He wagged his tail when I finally locked the cage door and turned my attention to him. I let my fearless basset out the back door. From a kitchen window, I watched him sniff his way around the swimming pool into another gnome garden. He didn't panic this time. He just sniffed red hats that resembled small fire hydrants, did his business and moved on. By the time I yelled for him to come back, he was out the open gate and had disappeared down the hill and out of sight.

I hurried around the swimming pool, past the pool house and giant barbeque, across the lawn, through the gnome garden and down several acres of grassy hillside. I finally caught a glimpse of Solow's long ears flying through the grass and followed, yelling for him to stop. He continued to race at basset speed after an animal bouncing through the high grass ahead of him.

The three of us careened down another hill and ended up on a path leading to an old house covered in dark shingles and shaded by a giant eucalyptus tree.

An older green compact car sat in patterns of shade.

Solow sniffed his way to the back of the house where I found him making friends with a cute little brown and white goat, young and possibly a miniature breed. The goat made friends with me right away, butting his furry head against my hip over and over until I pushed him away. Little Goat stood in front of a small replica of a traditional red barn, double doors at the bottom-front and a hayloft window under the peak of the seven-foot roof.

I peeked into the miniature goat barn, noticing an empty water bucket and empty food bin. The goat came up beside me and bawled something that probably meant "feed me" as he butted me gently. I found a faucet and filled the water bucket but came up empty on food possibilities.

Solow, Little Goat and I circled halfway around the house to the front door. The place looked too quiet and closed up to be lived in, but I climbed the three steps to the porch and knocked on the door anyway. I turned to leave, but turned back when I heard the door creak open. A pair of yellow-green eyes stared up at me. The door opened a bit more.

"Hi, I was just trying to get my dog, ah, Solow...."

"Hello. I'm the housekeeper...that is, I *was* the housekeeper for Mr. Hobblestone. Did you know him?" the young woman said in an Irish accent.

"No, just what I read in the newspaper. Very sad. Did you read the article in today's paper?" I asked.

"No, I don't get the paper, but I know all about the man since I worked for him for the last four years, I did. He had a touch of the arthritis, poor soul." She peeked out from strawberry blond curls falling into her milky-complexioned face. "He was a bit of a hermit, but a very nice one."

I figured I knew more about Henry than she, but it wasn't my business. "Is this his goat?" I pointed to the little guy who was getting a royal sniff-job from Solow.

"Oh yes. I'm so glad you found Willy, the little scamp. I would take him, but I live in a wee apartment in Salinas. In fact, I just started a new position, plus I am finishing up my training to be a nurse. As you can see, I have no time for goats."

"But you have time to straighten up Henry's house...."

"He would have wanted me to. The house will probably be sold, but he would not want anyone to see blood on the floor." Her face looked flushed.

"You mean, no one has cleaned things up since the accident?"

"I have just today found the time. My name is Breana Kinnicutt." She held out a dainty white hand. We shook hands.

"I'm Josephine Stuart, nice to meet you. I'm house sitting up the hill for the Trippys."

"Oh, for Lois, you are?"

"Yes. I guess Lois was a friend of Henry's."

"Yes, they knew one another. Henry had Lois trace'n his family, as people do, on the internet. She collected his information from time to time and looked up various ancestors." Breana opened the door wide. "Won't you come inside?"

"Thank you. Solow too?"

"Of course, the dear boy."

We swept into the front room. The little goat squeezed past us. Before I had time to grab him, he had his nose in a kitchen cupboard scarfing up a box of cheerios, box and all. I gripped his collar as he polished off the last of the cardboard and moved on to inhale a box of Girl Scout cookies. I tugged and pulled and eventually had him sequestered on the front porch.

"Willy looks hungry, he does. He never was one to eat grass like real goats." Breana searched the kitchen and came up with half a sack of oats. She poured the contents into a large bowl and carried it out to the porch. She closed the door and joined me at the window to watch the little fella eat his oats. We were all smiles and giggles until I happened to glance around at a dark stain on the hardwood floor in front of a large river rock fireplace.

"I didn't think it was possible to shoot oneself with a rifle," I said, trying to imagine such a feat.

"I didn't either, but what do I know about such things? People were not allowed to have weapons in Ireland, would you believe that? Now I wouldn't care to have one, really, I wouldn't." She stared at the floor for a moment. "I was very fond of old Henry, very much indeed. He told me stories about his life, and I told him what it was like to be Irish, livin' in Ireland."

"Can I help you clean up the mess?" I asked, looking around the disheveled living room.

"I will do the cleanin' for Henry. It's my duty, you see."

"By the way, who takes care of the goat?"

"Mother of God, I don't think anyone is takin' care of him, poor soul."

"Breana, about Henry's obituary, you really ought to read it."

"Was there a proper picture and all?"

"Yes, but you really need to read the article. I'll bring it down to you."

Breana cocked her head but didn't ask why I was so adamant about her reading a piece from the paper. I told her I would be back, and I would take charge of Willy temporarily. I said goodbye, and Breana closed the door behind me. Solow and I walked to the barn and found the goat drinking water. When he finally raised his head, his belly bulged on both sides, looking big enough to burst. He voluntarily waddled by my side along the path heading up to the Trippys' house.

A quarter of the way there, I heard a deep-throated motorcycle engine getting louder. Below us, back at Henry's house, a dusty black Harley Davidson motorcycle arrived in a cloud of gravel-dirt. A helmeted young man brushed himself off with gloved hands and entered the house. From a hundred yards away, I saw Breana embrace the man briefly, just before the front door closed.

David crossed my mind. I looked up at the heavens and wondered what he was doing at that moment.

Chapter Two

I planned to make another trip down the hill to see Breana, right after I prepared a temporary place for Willy to live. The Trippys' pool shack housed the pool heater and other pool equipment with enough room left on the concrete floor for a bed made of beach towels, a bucket of water and a food bowl.

Willy gave me a playful butt.

I rubbed his head and hoped he was happy in his temporary home.

I folded the newspaper article and stuffed it in my pocket, walked Solow to the other side of the pool, around the gnome village and through the gate. We rounded the house, and I hiked him into my pickup truck. Delighted to be traveling, he leaned left into my lap as I made a sharp right turn onto Langley Gulch Road, and two-hundred feet later made another right onto a gravel driveway leading to Henry's place, I hoped. The rusty excuse for a mailbox at the Langley end of the driveway had numbers on it but no name. A moment later, I relaxed when Henry's house came into view. I parked the truck behind Breana's green compact, the only vehicle around.

I helped Solow down from his seat. He leaned against my calf as I knocked on the front door, waited and then tried the doorknob. I pushed the door open and poked my head inside.

"Breana, it's Josephine, I brought the article for you to read! Are you here, Breana? Hellooo!" I walked inside. The place looked worse than when I left. Desk drawers, kitchen drawers and cupboard doors were all left open and the floor stain looked as dark and forbidding as ever. I shivered.

I moved through the house to a small bedroom featuring a single bed, a tall dark armoire, bed stand, lamp and a ragged braided rug on the wood floor. Obviously, Henry was not one for frills. Out of curiosity, I opened the wardrobe to see what kind of clothes he/she wore. To my great surprise, the furniture was home to a forty-inch flat screen TV and several stacks of paperback westerns.

I opened dresser drawers and found Henry's overalls, shirts, two jackets, socks and jockey shorts. There were no bras, no frilly stuff of any kind. I ran my hands under the clothing in the top drawer, then the second one and lastly the lowest drawer. On the bottom, toward the back of the drawer I felt cold smooth metal. I pulled out an oval-shaped gold locket attached to a trailing gold chain. I pried the locket open, and found two black and white pictures inside. One face resembled Henry's picture in the newspaper except much younger with long dark hair. I stared at the face, trying to imagine an older person with short white hair.

The second picture didn't ring any bells with me. The young man was a burly looking fellow with a mustache and twinkly eyes, the kind that roam. The faces looked to be close in age, in their twenties. *A handsome couple*, I thought. Who was this gal who pretended to be Henry? I slipped a fingernail between paper and gold and popped the picture free of its casing. On the back of the picture in flowery cursive it read, Henrietta M. Guthrie. I popped out the second picture, Byron P. Guthrie.

I heard a deep-throated rumble from a Harley coming up the drive. Gravel spattered the porch stairs. The engine went quiet just before Solow howled from his station at the front door. I quickly snapped the locket shut and dropped it in the back of the drawer. As I walked into the front room, Solow pushed against my leg and barked.

The front door opened.

"Josephine, what are you...? Mother of God, I forgot you were comin' back, I did. That must be your truck out there," Breana said, pulling a white helmet off her head of curls.

My cheeks felt hot. "I thought you were in the house so I sort of...came in to find you."

Breana didn't look too upset. "This is my friend, Nate."

Nate's excessive height and body mass contrasted greatly with Breana's small slim stature. He pulled off his black helmet, exposing a spiky black Mohawk and half a dozen ear-studs. He extended a gloved hand.

I shook the dusty glove, not wanting to look like a prude.

"I see you're giving the place a thorough cleaning," I said, rolling my eyes around the room.

"Actually, Breana lost her favorite bracelet here in the house somewhere. I'm helping her search for it," he smiled.

"Okay, well, I'll be going now. Oh, here's the article I wanted you to read." I handed it to Breana and stepped outside. Solow was at my heels, ready to say *adios*, and leave the young people to their secrets. The couple waved to us from the porch while we circled the eucalyptus tree and drove the short distance back to the Trippys' house.

Then, Solow and I went around the house to check on Willy and found him curled up on a chaise lounge. Without disturbing him, we rounded the pool, passed the dining room entrance and entered the house from the kitchen door.

I immediately dialed Lois. Her phone rang many times.

"Hello?" Lois answered.

"Wow, you sound sleepy," I said, wondering if she'd had too much to drink. "Sorry to bother you, but I need to know who's in charge of Henry's house now that he's gone. Things are kinda weird over there."

"Oh, this must be Josephine. Tom and I just fell asleep. It's 11:30 and we had a very busy day in Paris," she yawned.

"Sorry, I just need to know who to call about Henry's house."

"You called the right person. I'm looking after the place...except I can't do it right now," Lois giggled. "Just do what you can, Josephine. I'll be home in 29 days."

"Good night, Lois."

I called David.

He answered on the first ring. "Josie, honey, I was just thinking about you. Actually, you're on my mind a lot these days. Our Saturday night date was...."

"David, I have a situation over here...."

"You're not going to go solving other people's problems, are you?"

"Not if I can help it. The problem is that a couple of young people are going through Henry's stuff, his drawers, cupboards, everything. Supposedly, Breana lost her bracelet somewhere in the house—she's the housekeeper—*was*, anyway...."

"Let me get this straight. Henry is the guy who died and left his bird to the Trippys."

"Right, only Henry is actually *Henrietta* and the bird came with a goat."

"Okay, you said Henrietta had a housekeeper named Breana and she lost her bracelet."

"I don't know if she lost anything. All I know is that she and her boyfriend are digging through all of Henry…etta's things. What right do they have? I wish I knew who the relatives are so I could let them know what's going on."

"Wish I could help, sweetheart. These kittens are a full time job right now. Know anyone who needs a kitten?" he groaned.

"Nope, and don't try to talk me into one." I made a peanut butter sandwich while we talked.

"And Harley's bringing Monica over to my house next month because he's going on a cruise with her nanny. I think it's getting serious. Have you met Emily?"

"No, I hav…."

"Boris wants a cracker."

"Hold your horses!" I said.

"You want me to hold my what?" David asked.

"Not you, the bird. Boris knows way too many words."

"Boris wants a cracker."

"David, I have to go now. Talk to you soon." I hung up.

It was already mid-afternoon and I'd promised my best friend and number one painter that I would go to a matinee with her. Alicia's husband, Ernie, and their ten-year-old son, Trigger, were winding up a camping trip in Ben Lomond with the Watsonville Cub Scouts.

I left Solow with Willy in the backyard, and called my friend to let her know I was on my way. I drove out of Prunedale using the back roads, made a quick stop at the feed store for a sack of alfalfa pellets for the goat, and arrived at Alicia's Watsonville lake-front home twenty minutes later. We had time for a cup of tea in Alicia's sunny kitchen before the movie started at four.

"Josephine, are you sure you have your facts straight? How could this Henrietta pretend to be a man for all those years?"

"Do you have today's *Sentinel*?"

"Sure, right over there by the fireplace." She fetched the paper.

"The obits."

Alicia found the page and read the article. "Okay, I see what you mean. What about the people searching the place?"

"They seem nice enough, but they're definitely snooping around, looking for something. Did I tell you I'm taking care of a goat?"

"No. Why would you do that?"

"He was Henry's and he's very friendly. He's a cute little guy and so far no one's seeing that he has food and water or anything. I don't know much about goats, except that they supposedly eat everything in sight."

"How's David?"

"Playing *nervous father* to four baby kittens," I giggled as we headed outside to my truck for a quick ride to the movie theater. "Allie, are you happy to be going back to work Tuesday?"

"Sure, banking hours always agree with me," she laughed, as we motored across town. "Why can't we paint before ten?"

"The owner closes the restaurant and bar at two in the morning and doesn't want to open the doors for us any sooner than ten. And the restaurant is closed Sunday and Monday, and he doesn't want to be disturbed. I understand how he feels."

"Jo, have you heard the rumors that the Crazy Horse is haunted?"

"Really? Who told you that?"

"I read an article in the paper about a year ago. They wrote about Brookdale Lodge and a few other ghostly establishments, but it seems most of the ghosts live in San Juan Bautista. The reporter talked about people seeing a lady wearing a long red dress coming down the stairs at the Crazy Horse. In the old days, it was a brothel. They figure she was the Madam," Alicia laughed.

I pulled into an empty parking place and cut the engine.

"Jo, you're not afraid of ghosts, are you?"

"If a ghost appears while we're there, I'll probably toss my paint and run. What about you, Allie?"

"I'm not saying I'm brave, but I don't think a ghost would hurt anyone, least of all two fast-runners like us," she giggled.

We walked up to the front entrance of the Green Valley Theater, paid for our tickets and hurried inside, passing three long lines at the concession counter and up the hallway to screen number four. Most of the seats were taken, but we finally found a pair of empty tenth-row seats in the very middle. The movie was already under way as we squeezed past a family of super-sized young gents and their mama. We made ourselves comfortable behind a wiggly little girl and her two popcorn-crunching brothers.

Suddenly, I remembered Boris.

"Oh, no."

Half a dozen heads in front of us turned.

"Jo, what's the matter?" Alicia whispered.

"I just remembered that I'm babysitting a big bird and a goat. Solow is always fine when I'm gone, but I'm not sure about Big Beak and little Willy. What if the goat falls in the swimming pool and can't swim?" I whispered over high-octane engines, thunder and creepy music.

Heads swiveled back to the screen.

"Do we need to leave?" Alicia asked, looking concerned.

"No, but we should go straight home after the movie." I looked at the screen, trying to let go of a nagging feeling that Willy had somehow swallowed all the water in the pool while Boris had unlatched his cage door and ransacked the house. The images from my imagination were much more real that the chaos on the screen. I rubbed the back of my neck and closed my eyes.

"Jo, you look uncomfortable. Let's go."

"Are you sure, Allie?"

She nodded. We collected our purses and sweaters and gingerly worked our way past protruding knees belonging to grumpy patrons. A box of popcorn hit the floor followed by expletives aimed at my back.

Alicia and I left the movie house, along with our plans to dine at the Nifty Fifty across the parking lot from the theater. The casual restaurant was decked out with old stuff to make old people think they were young again. I liked the place because it was clean and the food was good.

Babysitting was beginning to be a bother, but I had given my word to Lois and Breana, so I dropped Alicia at her house and sped back to the white carpets of Prunedale.

I curbed my truck by the front door. Solow howled from the backyard, as I stood on the porch digging through my purse for the house key. I found it, turned the key and marched through the house carrying a twenty-pound sack of alfalfa pellets under one arm. I entered the kitchen ready to read Boris the riot act.

"Boris wants a cracker."

"Hi, big bird, you look like you're doing fine," I said, feeling the knots in my neck loosen. I glanced at his food and water. He didn't need anything. I leaned the sack of pellets against the door, found a soda cracker and gave it to Boris just because he hadn't caused trouble while I was away. We chatted a bit; he screeched, I talked. Finally, he unfluffed his feathers, looked me in the eye and cooed, "I wuv you, pretty bird."

"I love you too, Boris."

"Stuff it!"

"I can't believe you just said that…well, you are a dumb bird. I'm sure you don't know what you're talking about." I picked up the sack and headed outside. Willy and Solow stood by the back door waiting to greet me. What a wonderful welcome home. I was smiling right up to the moment when I stuck my head into the pool house door. Willy had shredded all the beach towels. Ka-ching! I saw my five-hundred-dollar check from Lois diminishing before my eyes.

As I walked around the pool looking for trouble, I noticed a pile of pellet-type poop on the concrete, obviously a gift from Willy. I searched the pool house and found a broom and dustpan. As I swept up goat mess, I heard footsteps behind me.

"Hi, Josephine, what are you doin'?" Breana asked as she walked around the pool.

"Just cleaning up after Willy. Have you been here before?"

"Oh, yes, Lois and I loved to visit and chat about the silliest of things. I see that Willy is happy, bless his heart," she smiled.

"Yeah and he's hardly gotten into trouble." Even as I said it, I imagined a hundred more terrible things he might do in the future. "Can I help you with something? Did you find your bracelet?"

"My what? Oh, me bracelet, I'm afraid not." Breana stroked Solow's head and his long velvety ears, putting him into a love trance. My basset was generally a good judge of character but could be swayed by offers of food and attention.

"Would you like to come inside for a cup of tea?"

"T'would be ever so nice. Thank you, Josephine."

We stepped into the kitchen. I plugged in the teapot and searched the pantry for snacks, unable to remember my long ago peanut butter sandwich. It was almost seven and my stomach rumbled. I thought about burgers at the Nifty Fifty and kicked myself for worrying about Boris and Willy.

Breana sat down at the kitchen table. "Isn't this lovely," she gushed as I served a plate of tuna on crackers with our green tea. "I just love Lois' taste in china."

"Boris wants a cracker."

I rolled my eyes and stuck a loaded cracker between the wires.

Boris latched onto it with his beak.

"I didn't know he liked tuna," Breana said, wide-eyed.

"I didn't either," I shrugged. "Did you read the article from the *Sentinel*?"

"That's one reason I'm here. 'Twas an interestin' bit—I'm havin' a hard time believin' it, I am. Henry was such a gentleman, not one to do female things, you see. He would not wash his own dishes, never wore anything but plaid shirts and denim overalls. But he did have his modest-private side. Once I caught him watching a soap opera on the telly. He claimed he was just flippin' through the programs. Of course, I believed him then. Now I wonder." Her voice trailed off as Boris asked for a cracker.

"Does he really want a cracker or is he just talking?" I asked.

"He likes anything crunchy, and if you want him to quiet down, give him a cup of chamomile tea. He's really not such a bad fellow if you talk to him occasionally."

I didn't see Breana giving the bird any attention, maybe because Solow wouldn't leave her side.

"Josephine, since you're actin' on Lois' behalf, I came to ask a favor of you...."

"Sure, what's on your mind?"

"Today I found out that the apartment I told you about won't be ready for another month. They're havin' trouble removin' the current resident, they are. I was wonderin' if I might be able to stay in Henry's house until..."

"You're saying I can make decisions about the house?" I scratched my head and Boris clawed his topknot. "If it's really up to me, I don't see why not...."

"Oh thank you, Josephine. You don't know what this means to me." She excused herself and headed out the back door. Through the window, I watched her circle the pool, pass through the gate and disappear down the hill, leaving me wondering how I had inherited such authority in all things Henry.

Chapter Three

Monday morning I woke up to birds chirping. On second thought, it sounded like Boris was carrying on a conversation with himself. He generally added a squawk or two between sentences. I decided to rest my bones a little longer and ignore his prattle. It was my last day off for a while—might as well enjoy it a few more minutes.

After a long shower and a light breakfast, Solow and I went outside to check on Willy. We found him stretched out on his favorite lawn furniture, the posh purple chaise lounge, two legs splayed over the side. He heard us and instantly the boys began playing dog and goat games like who can run the fastest and who can jump the highest. Of course, Willy had it all over Solow. After all, he was still young, frisky and untrained. Too bad he was leaving his messes on the concrete surrounding the pool instead of on the wide swath of lawn bordering the concrete.

I grabbed a broom and dustpan from the pool house, swept up a pile of pellet-looking stuff and walked it over to the garbage can. I flipped the lid back. I poured the...oops. As the pellets rolled and fell into the can, I noticed a glint of blue light coming from the bottom of the can...a piece of glass maybe. Instantly, I worried about Willy eating sharp objects that might hurt his tummy. Something looked shiny and needed to be investigated.

Solow stayed at my side, competing with the bouncy goat for my attention.

I entered the house, took one sheet of Boris' newspaper and spread it on the patio. As I tipped the garbage can on its rim, pellets of poop rolled onto the paper. I re-entered the house and came back with one of Lois' lovely dinner knives. I stabbed at the partially-covered object until the pellets of interest fell away, revealing a heavy gold-colored ring with a flat, quarter-inch circle of blue stone on top. I balanced the bulky ring on the end of the knife and carried it inside to the kitchen sink.

My heart thumped wildly as I ran hot water and a glob of detergent over the ring. I worked suds into the golden grooves with my fingers until it was mostly clean. The cleaner it got, the older it looked.

I ran a fingernail around a groove in the metal, getting the last bit of grunge out. The glass moved a tiny bit—did I hear a tiny pop? I pressed upward and the whole top of the ring hinged straight up. "What in the world?"

"Boris wants a cracker."

"Shhh...I'm thinking."

"Squawk!"

I noticed the ring was hollow under the glass lid. Actually, the glass cleaned up real nice, no scratches at all, and the most beautiful cobalt blue I'd ever seen. I loved using cobalt blue in my paintings, especially after reading about the Impressionists. Being rather poor, Auguste Renoir was thrilled to have a little pot of cobalt blue in his assortment of colors, as it was the most brilliant of colors—and most expensive.

The big question on my mind was: how did Willy get hold of the ring? Why did he eat it? I thought back to the starving little fellow—no food until Breana gave him the bowl of oats. Did a ring fall into the sack of oats? Not likely, but it would be a good hiding place for a ring. Why would someone want to hide a silly old ring? I made a mental note to show the trinket to a friend of a friend at The Jewelry Company in San Juan Bautista.

I wasn't ready to share my discovery with anyone else yet, not until I knew more about the ring. What if it was stolen property—or worse—a carrier of poison? The thought made me shiver. I searched through drawers and cupboards around the kitchen for a safe place to keep the bulky old ring. I tried it on my ring finger. It twirled around and fell off. I tried my middle and index fingers—still too loose.

The doorbell chimed.

To be on the safe side, I quickly dropped the ring into Lois' charming little sugar bowl and rushed through the house to open the front door. It was a nice surprise. I hadn't seen David in a week. He looked better than ever—tall and trim—with thick salt and pepper hair and a grin that gave me a heat rash.

"Come in. How did you escape the kittens?"

His embrace was heavenly. "Alicia called me. Said she was a little worried about you with all the animal responsibilities you've taken on. She said she'd watch the kittens if I wanted to visit you—so here I am! Is everything okay?"

"Everything's fine. I feel bad that I worried her. You know my imagination."

"Oh, yeah!" he laughed. "And I'm imagining...."

"I am too, but first I want you to meet Boris and Willy." I took David's hand and led him to the kitchen.

"Back up!" Boris instructed, giving David the *cockatoo evil eye,* head cocked, head feathers flared.

David laughed.

"Back up. Now!" he said, adding a loud screech for good measure.

"Boris wants a cracker?" I asked as I headed for the cracker box on the counter. I quickly handed over a saltine and Boris became his alter ego, *Nice Bird*.

"Let's go see the goat," David said, taking my hand and pulling me toward the back door. We stepped outside.

"More gnomes?" he laughed, looking beyond the pool.

"Yeah, Solow isn't too fond of them but somebody around here loves gnomes. There's a whole collection of wooden gnomes in the den and little glass ones in five bathrooms. There's even a gnome in the laundry room."

"You know the house pretty well—at least the gnome sections," he teased. But he was right. I had spent a little time in every room, enjoying Trippy memorabilia from their trips around the world. Seems they spent a lot of time in Gnomeland.

David gently squeezed my hand as we crossed the patio. Willy and Solow napped on the lawn until they heard our laughter and perked up their ears. Together they circled us with waggy tails, ma-ahing and barking. It looked like Solow finally had the brother he'd always wanted. Fortunately, the patio and sidewalks were clear of pellets and pooh. After the love-fest with the boys, we went back inside for some quality time of our own.

Later, we decided to go for a walk and pick up some lunch in Prunedale. We walked down the driveway and made a right onto Langley Gulch Road. After walking about five minutes, we turned left on San Miguel Canyon, the main road through town, and hoofed our way to the local shopping center and La Tapatia Restaurant for lunch. Except for a familiar looking black Harley, the side parking area was empty.

We walked inside. Obviously, the lunch rush was over, but one young couple sat and talked at a table near the back. David followed me and my curiosity to the occupied table.

"Saints alive, if it isn't Josephine!" she cried when she saw me. "You remember my friend...Nate?" Her cheeks turned pink.

"Breana, this is my friend, David...." I said.

"Have a seat, man," Nate said, pointing to a couple of chairs opposite the cozy couple.

We sat down. "Have you found your bracelet yet, Breana?"

"No, but I'm sure it's around somewhere, and now that I'll be stayin' at Henry's for a month, I'll have time to look for it. A gift from me grandmamma, it was." She turned her head and smiled at Nate.

"Breana was Henry's housekeeper," I explained to David, "and she'll be staying in his house for a month, until her new apartment is ready." *And why would she wear her beloved bracelet to do housework at Henry's?* I wondered.

A waitress arrived with a bill for Nate and two menus for us. We ordered without opening them. When ordering Mexican food, I always ordered fish tacos and David consistently chose chili verde.

"Looks like you two do this a lot," Nate laughed. "Breana and I are just getting tah know each other, know what I mean?" he said in a slow, easy-going way.

Breana's cheeks reddened.

Nate excused himself, walked over to the bar and made a phone call. When he came back a couple of minutes later, Breana's cheeks were still red.

"By the way, Breana, what happened to Henry's gun?" I asked her. "I didn't see it around anywhere. Don't people generally mount them over the fireplace?" Without looking at him, I imagined David rolling his eyes.

"Josie, you're thinking of the old western movies…."

"Well, if you saw Henry's house, you would be thinking *old western* too," I added.

"Actually, the Sheriff's deputies took the gun. They wanted to make sure it was the same one that…well, you know," said Breana. She glanced at the napkin on her lap. "It's all quite strange. They have me totally foxed."

"Call me curious," I said, "but did Henry have a will?"

I glanced at David's scowl. He obviously thought I was snooping into things I should leave alone. Actually, everyone at the table looked uncomfortable.

"No one has found a will—we really don't know," she said as all the rosy color drained from her face. I watched her eyes wander across the room, pausing at the front door.

The waitress took Nate's money.

"Bree, time to go," he said as he grabbed his shiny black helmet from a chair at the next table. "Nice meetin' y'all," he said to David.

Breana picked up a white helmet, and off they went. We heard them circle the building, and watched through the window as they roared onto San Miguel, Breana's arms wrapped tightly around Nate's black leather jacket.

We finished our lunch and hiked all the way back to the Trippys' house. A taxi would have been nice, but no such thing existed in Prunedale. We must have burned ten thousand calories each, since most of the return trip was up hill—the long Trippy driveway being the steepest of all. David said goodbye at the front door, explaining he needed to get home so that Alicia could get back to her family.

As soon as David drove away in his little black Miata, I called Alicia's cell phone to let her know that David was on his way. She said the kittens were doing fine now that she had made a place for them inside a laundry basket. Fluffy seemed to think it was a good idea too. Containing the four hungry little fluff balls worked in her favor. Alicia claimed that with a little time to herself, Fluffy had become a nicer cat.

Nicer cat? I didn't buy that, after all the times she'd coaxed Solow into futile cat chases. Solow's short legs were no match for Fluffy and she knew it. But Solow, being a typical guy, always took the bait. He had his pride, did the chase and always suffered *loser's humiliation*.

"Allie, I really appreciate you helping out today so that David and I could spend some time together."

"Did he ask the question…I mean, how was your afternoon?"

"Great, really nice. What question, Allie?"

"He had me watch the kittens because he said he had something he wanted to ask you. I just thought it might be important…."

"You thought he was going to propose. Well, he didn't, but it was a very nice afternoon." We hung up. I suddenly felt like the wonderful afternoon was less wonderful than it had been before talking to Alicia. But maybe no proposal was best since I didn't feel quite ready for another round of matrimony.

My marriage to Marty had ended when he was run over by an eighteen-wheeler about seventeen years ago. I had adjusted my life accordingly, but when I thought about him, I still felt a lump in my throat after all those years.

The house phone rang. I grabbed it on the second ring.

"Josephine, this is Breana. Something terrible has happened...."

"Breana, what happened? Are you okay?"

"I'm okay—it's Henry's house! I know it was a bit of a mess when you saw it, but it's ten times the worse now! Holy Saints be with us," she sobbed. "Thank God, Henry isn't here to see it, bless his soul."

"I'll be right down!" I hung up the phone, dashed out the back door, through the gate and down the first hill with Solow and Willy at my heels. I imagined the worst. As we careened down the second hill, I focused on the distant house below, draped in dark shingles. The outside looked unharmed. We sprinted up the stairs to the front door—a quick knock and we burst into the living room.

Breana was at a loss for words. She motioned with her hand, waving it around the room, her mouth open, cheeks wet. The room had been severely disarranged, pulled apart, but the kitchen was the worst.

"Looks like someone opened every drawer in the house. Is that flour all over the floor?"

Breana nodded. "They emptied all the canisters—rice, sugar, even a box of Rice Crispies! Henry's favorite."

"Where's Nate?"

"Nate dropped me off in front of the house and left. This is what I found," she shivered. "Maybe we should put the animals out...."

"You're right, before they eat everything on the floor." I grabbed Willy by the back of his neck and hauled him outside. Solow followed, always wanting to be *included* with his adopted brother. They already had white powder on their faces ear to ear, and up to their ankles.

I closed the front door and attended to Breana and her shivering. She said she'd planned to move her possessions into Henry's house the next day. But since the fiendish attack, she couldn't think clearly.

I rounded up a broom, an old Hoover upright and a bottle of window cleaner. Breana was a housekeeper by trade, but she obviously needed a jump-start.

"Breana, you'll feel better if you stay busy— cleaning, that is." I parked the vacuum cleaner in front of her. "I'll be right back." I ducked into the bedroom to check on the locket. I found three empty drawers upside down on the floor. After several minutes of pawing through piles of clothing, I gave up the search. The locket could have been found by Breana and Nate before the house was tossed or it could have been found by the mysterious ransacker-creep.

Breana straightened the living room while I worked on the kitchen. I wiped gunk off the counters onto the floor, then swept it all into a dustpan, dumping the flour-coated contents into a garbage can, over and over until squares of linoleum finally appeared. Several attacks with a wet mop brought out the shine. Once the living room and kitchen were presentable, I worked the bedroom, ever conscious of a missing locket.

Breana scrubbed the bathroom.

From the bedroom window, I noticed the sun was about to set. It was getting late, and I still needed to drive to my home in Aromas, pack up paint supplies and ladders and drive back to the Trippy house for the night.

"Breana, I need to go. What are your plans for tonight?"

"Don' be worryin' over me, Josephine. I feel much better now. I'll just drive back to my apartment in Salinas. Do you mind if we leave at the same time?" She shivered.

"Not at all." I rounded up Willy and Solow while Breana gathered her purse, keys and a book. She jumped into her little car, circled the eucalyptus and sped away.

The playful boys and I trudged up the hillside. The journey seemed ten times longer and darker than the earlier downhill version. I followed behind the boys, knowing that their vision at dusk was better than mine.

Hungry and tired, we finally walked through the pool gate onto terra firma. I poured fresh food and water for Willy, as twinkly stars began to appear.

Solow and I dragged ourselves into the kitchen. I flipped the light switch.

"What in Sam Hill?" Boris crabbed.

"Boris better be a good boy or no cracker."

"Boris wants a cracker."

"Give me a break...."

"Squawk!"

I ignored the following unintelligible bird chatter because I was hungry and so was Solow. I made short work of a bowl of Campbell's soup and Solow horsed down his bowl of kibble. We then hustled out to the truck and headed for home.

Fifteen minutes later, we cruised up Otis Road and parked in front of my house. Using a flashlight from the glove compartment, I inserted my house key and opened the front door.

Solow ran to the kitchen to see if any food had fallen to the floor while we were gone. I gathered sketches, photos, camera and three sets of painting clothes, stuffed everything into a suitcase, rolled it out to the truck and hoisted it all into the bed. From there, I aimed my flashlight at the path circling to the back of the house and my tin shed.

Dark and decaying, black widow spiders loved my shed. I flashed the light into every corner, every place the wicked spiders might hide. Carefully, I reached inside the ten-by-ten structure and pulled a box of paint cans out of the shed, then went back for my red plastic tackle box full of plastic bottles of acrylic paint. Next, I pulled out a stack of folded tarps, a level and a bucket full of paint brushes. I stacked everything in my handy wheelbarrow and pushed it over to the truck.

After two more trips to the shed for ladders, I loaded everything into the truck bed, pulled the metal Snugtop down tight and hoisted Solow into the passenger seat. I took a last look around the house, locked the door and drove back to Prunedale with Solow at my side. He seemed unusually needy, or maybe he was confused as to which house he would be living in. Or maybe he was nervous—sensing something in our future.

I dreamt about spiders, big female spiders all shiny black with hungry eyes and red patches on their round bellies. Several of them stood shoulder to shoulder doing the can-can. Their red bellies jiggled to the music coming from the pool house where Willy ran his sewing machine-music maker contraption.

My nightmare ended suddenly when a loud screech from the kitchen pulled me awake. I blinked my eyes and listened for a moment.

"Back up, now!" Boris growled.

I wondered if he too was having a nightmare. Do cockatoos talk in their sleep?

Chapter Four

It was no surprise Tuesday morning, waking up to Boris cock-a-doodle-dooing like a crazed rooster. I was getting used to his shenanigans. The deranged bird had no regard for my quality of life or sleep, or Solow's. The poor basset looked at me with blood-shot eyes as I peeked out from under a white ruffled duvet. He buried his head under his fat front paws.

I listened to a few more cock-a-doodle-doos and decided Boris was actually very good at doing imitations.

I did an imitation of an angry house sitter as I stomped into the kitchen.

"Boris wants a crack...."

"I know, I know...." I handed him a saltine. "You want me to be nice to you? Then let me sleep, okay?" I gave Mr. Big Beak fresh water and food, as morning light from the east windows brightened the room.

Boris ignored me, holding the cracker with his talons, biting off pieces with the curved point of his large beak.

I let Solow out the back door. Just as the door swung shut, I heard a cock-a-doodle-doo. I looked back at Boris, the last of the cracker disappearing into his mouth.

"You are good!" I said to the handsome bird. "Unbelievable."

I put Mr. Coffee to work and headed down the hall to sweet silence under a hot shower. I dried off and pulled on an old t-shirt and cut-off shorts covered in paint smears. Sometimes my clothes became so stiff with paint they had to be thrown in the garbage because no charitable organization would accept my donation. To make up for ugly clothes, I always gave special attention to my hair, makeup and jewelry, hoping I wouldn't be mistaken for a bag lady.

After breakfast, I made a mental check on things stowed in the truck. Hopefully, I had packed everything. A twenty-minute drive southeast on Highway 129 took me to San Juan Bautista, home of one of the best cared for missions in California. The small downtown area was ten times bigger than Aromas, but still small and charming. Dozens of storefronts had not been changed since the Lincoln administration, still decorated with false fronts, outside balconies and quaint signage. It was a commingling of Wild West and Spanish architecture.

I checked my watch—right on time at ten o'clock. I curbed the truck in the middle of town, behind Alicia's green Volvo, in front of the painted brick exterior of the Crazy Horse Saloon. The owner of the restaurant, Alonzo Alvarez, had left the front door unlocked for us. As Alicia and I entered the ancient two-story building, the owner descended a narrow staircase off to our right and greeted us warmly.

A jazzy tune poured from Alonzo's pocket. He excused himself, answered his cell phone and headed back up the stairs.

Alicia and I hauled our equipment into the street-level, ancient, high-ceilinged dining area. On the last trip to the truck, I handed her the stack of folded tarps while I carried the little five-foot ladder and paint box. It took a minute for our eyes to adjust to the dim indoor lighting, consisting of a series of antique railroad lanterns attached to the walls and fitted with dim light bulbs. The dark wooden walls had three large framed-in areas housing three faded and distressed paintings of saloon girls, each picture four-feet high and eight-feet wide.

Alicia and I had been hired to replace the old-time paintings with a bucking horse scene on the south wall behind the bar, and two companion paintings on the west wall—a cattle stampede and the San Juan Bautista Mission with Father Junipero Serra leading a flock of Indian children. The subject ideas came from Alonzo's collection of Old West picture books.

Obviously young, ambitious and innovative, Alonzo had recently inherited the Crazy Horse building from a great aunt who adored him.

"Alonzo is pretty easy on the eyes," Alicia laughed, setting the tarps down on the floor. "Ouch, there was something prickly in those tarps!"

I pushed the paint box against the wall as I babbled on about Alonzo. "And he's very easy to work with. He listened to my ideas and I listened to his. We agreed on a bucking horse picture, a Father Serra picture and a Wild West landscape with cattle. One problem, the saloon girls were supposed to be painted out before we arrived. Guess we'll have to do it ourselves. Allie, the blue tape is over there in the canvas bag. You tape the frames and I'll mix up a neutral sky-blue color that we can use in all three pictures for continuity."

"I'm on it, boss," Alicia said, rubbing her arm. "I'll use the six-foot ladder."

I mixed up a muted blue, set my five-foot ladder in place and began painting over the scantily dressed gal behind the bar, inching the ladder forward now and then. Alicia painted over a dance hall girl playing cards with some tough-looking whiskered characters. I finished blanking out the first painting and moved on to the third—a woman wearing a strapless dress. Half the picture was indiscernible—a patchwork of stains and faded shapes.

Alicia finished covering her assigned painting and then helped me finish mine.

Alonzo appeared. "Looks better already," he laughed.

"Alicia and I are going to walk around town for at least half an hour to make sure this paint is dry before we draw on it. If I can borrow the Old West books, I'll have copies made of the pictures you like."

"They're right here," Alonzo said, picking up the two large coffee table books. I took one; Alicia took the other.

Warm air, light traffic and a few red hens set the scene in historic San Juan Bautista. We headed south along the uneven concrete sidewalk, passing rustic shop after shop—a clock shop, music shop, Mexican restaurant, gallery, jewelry store, bakery, ice cream shop, Mexican restaurant. We crossed the street and headed north—clothing boutique, lamp shop, Mexican restaurant, junk shop, metal sculpture, sundries, photo gallery, coffee shop, Mexican restaurant and eventually a stationary shop with a copy machine.

I made one eight-by-ten color copy of each of the three pictures. In my sketches, I had changed various subjects enough that the paintings could not be called copies of someone else's work, and our painting styles would cinch it. The bucking horse would have a livery stable and an oak tree behind it, instead of the original prairie and cacti. Father Serra's face would be cloaked and hidden as he walked toward the mission, followed by a stream of Indian children—half the number in the original painting, plus a couple of playful goats. The landscape full of cattle would have fewer cows and trees and more dry gulch.

Alicia volunteered to paint the most complicated picture, Father Serra and the Indians. She was comfortable painting people and animals. I would begin with the horse picture and end with the landscape. I estimated the project would take about twelve work days if all went as planned. Alonzo wanted us out of the building every day by five o'clock because that was happy hour and the beginning of the dinner hour.

Two old cronies watched from their bar stools as Alicia and I walked into the dining room. Alonzo introduced his two frappé-drinking friends. I tried to forget that they were watching me work, their eyes glued to my backside as I stood on the third rung of my ladder drawing the bucking horse, erasing parts of him and trying again and again to get the proportions just right.

Alicia drew her complicated scene onto the freshly painted, framed-in rectangle on the west wall. I trusted her to do a fantastic job because she had natural talent enhanced by an art degree. Ever humble, she was once a little street urchin in Tijuana, later adopted by an American family. Her ten-year-old son, Trigger, and her professor of biology husband, Ernie, were two of my favorite guys, right up there with my dad and David.

Alicia walked up beside me and whispered, "Jo, I don't feel very good."

I looked into her pale, sweaty face and knew something was very wrong. I automatically put my hand to her forehead. No fever. "Let's go outside for a minute." We went out into the bright daylight blinking and worried.

"Why are you holding your arm like that?"

"I don't know, it aches and feels hot." She turned and pulled her sleeve up.

"Bull's eye! You have a bull's eye on your arm. What happened? Allie, you better sit down here on the curb."

She sat down gingerly and leaned her head forward.

"Are you going to be sick?"

"I don't think so. I just don't feel well. I'm sorry, Jo, I don't think I can paint today."

"Don't worry about that. I'm going to drive you home right now." I walked back into the building and explained the situation to Alonzo. He helped me carry all my equipment to the truck, asking if there was anything else he could do. As I pulled the Snugtop down, I caught sight of a spider moving fast across the stack of tarps.

"Allie, do you know anything about spider bites?"

"Not really. I've been lucky so far...." Her eyes widened and her jaw dropped.

"I think your luck won't help you this time. I just saw a spider," I said as I helped her into the passenger seat. "That big red circle on your arm looks like a spider bite to me." I wasn't about to tell her what I really thought—that the bite was from a black widow. It was too scary to think, let alone to say out loud.

I rounded the truck, climbed in and we headed through town onto Highway 129 to Watsonville. It was all I could do to keep calm. My heart raced. I hadn't said the "black widow" word to Alicia yet, but I was thinking it. It was my fault. I should have bug-bombed the shed before I pulled stuff out.

Instead of taking Alicia home, I decided to take her to the closest Doc-in-a-Box without telling her until we were there. She wouldn't have a clue where we were going since she was curled up in a ball with her eyes closed.

As we sailed down the highway, my foot naturally pushed hard on the accelerator. My mind was so full of spiders it had no room for speed limits and rules of the road. A CHP on a motorcycle stationed behind a grove of oak trees aimed his speeder machine at us as we passed. I saw him and let off the gas but it was too late. He burst out from his shady hideout, red and blue lights flashing.

I pulled over.

Alicia raised her head.

"Sorry, Allie. Guess I might have been going too fast. Can you reach my paperwork in the glove compartment?"

A lanky young officer bent down and looked past me to Alicia. She handed the papers to me to hand to him.

He barely looked at them. "Ma'am, is there something wrong?"

"I'm okay...I think...."

"Officer, she was bitten by a black widow. That's why I was speeding. I'm taking her to the Doc-in-the-Box on Green Valley Road."

Alicia gasped. "A black widow?"

"Sorry, Allie, I didn't want to scare you."

"Follow me, ladies." He walked back to his motorcycle, gave it a kick and roared past us, lights flashing. I fired up the truck and eventually caught up to his bike. We traveled at the speed limit, way too slow for me. Finally we turned up Green Valley Road, motored five blocks and entered the parking area. The officer slid off his Harley and motioned for me to park in a blue-lined "handicap" parking space, the only place available.

I don't know why the officer followed us inside: distrust, duty, a caring attitude or the fact that Alicia was an unusually beautiful woman.

Alicia leaned on my arm as we approached the front desk.

"Here, fill these out and drop them over there," the prune-faced receptionist pointed to a full tray at the end of the counter.

"How long until my friend can see a doctor?" I glanced back at the officer standing by the front door. Every seat was taken and almost every lap had a baby on it.

Prune-lips checked her watch. "We have two doctors on duty and a well-baby lecture starting in five minutes. I'd say forty-five minutes, maybe...."

"We need something faster than that," I said, shoving the papers back to Miss Prune. I pulled on Alicia's sleeve to follow me, since she seemed to be zoned out and in a world of hurt on some other planet.

"Ow!"

"Oh, sorry Allie, that's your sore arm."

The officer saw us coming and pulled his helmet down over thinning blond hair. "Watsonville Hospital?" he asked.

I nodded, "Where else?" and followed him across town. The big blue hospital building never looked so good. I curbed the truck outside the emergency entrance—next to Blondie's motorcycle. I had to practically pull Alicia out of the truck. The minute her feet hit the pavement, she threw up.

"God forgive me," I whispered. But guilt would have to wait. I had to get Alicia to a doctor immediately. I had heard stories of black widow bites and they weren't pleasant. Thankfully, Alicia was only 35-years-old and healthy. Plus, I heard somewhere that it was unusual for a person to die from a bite.

I left Alicia sitting on a bench outside the emergency entrance, and hurried into the building, carrying our purses and looking around for help. I tapped my foot impatiently at the front desk waiting for the nurse to get off the phone.

The CHP Officer walked into the room with Alicia in his arms. He gently set her down in a chair and then talked to a male nurse at the front desk. We were assured that Alicia would be called as soon as possible. I noticed there were half a dozen other people sitting patiently in plastic chairs with emergency health problems.

"Ladies, please excuse me, I need to go catch some speeders," he chuckled and wished Alicia good luck.

"Allie, will you be all right—I need to get you registered?"

"Go ahead, Jo."

I gave the clean-shaven nurse Alicia's health card, driver's license, spa card, Macy's card and library card. In return, he handed me a batch of paperwork on a clipboard for her to fill out. I went back to my chair. Between the two of us, we completed the forms and I turned them in. Half an hour had passed and all the same people were still sitting, hurting, waiting.

Finally, I had time to call Allie's husband Ernie. He answered the phone and said he and Trigger would meet us at the hospital in ten minutes. Less than ten minutes later, he bolted into the emergency waiting room. I'd never seen Alicia's handsome Hispanic husband pale-faced and teary-eyed before.

She went limp in his arms.

Trigger sat down in a chair next to me. One look at his scared little face and I knew I had to hold back my tears. I had to be strong for Trigger.

Forty-five minutes later, the nurse called for Alicia Quintana.

Ernie walked with her to an assigned cubicle with no walls, just rainbow curtains. More time passed.

I had no more fingernails to chew, so I found a vending machine, a Snickers bar for Trigger and a cup of coffee for me. On my way back to the waiting room,

I passed by the rainbow room, pausing to count shoes. I counted only one pair and they belonged to Ernie. Feeling frantic, I cruised by the front counter and asked the nurse if a doctor was on the way. In a voice suitable for three-year-olds, he explained that there were people ahead of my friend. I took the hint, grabbed a magazine and went back to my chair.

Minutes later, I looked up in time to see a doctor slip between the rainbow curtains.

After ten minutes with the doc, the Quintanas were back in the waiting room.

"Well, what did the doctor say?"

Ernie looked somewhat relieved as he double checked a handful of paperwork that included a prescription and a list of do's and don'ts. "She can take aspirin for pain and this prescription for an antivenin. He already gave her a shot of it to get things started. The doctor said she'd have to *ride it out*, and to come in if there were any complications." He held up a long list of possible complications.

I walked with the family to Ernie's Toyota Camry and stood by the driver's door while he helped Alicia into the passenger seat. When Ernie came around to the driver's side, I whispered how sorry I was for neglecting to eradicate the black widows.

He hugged me and told me not to worry.

Trigger waved goodbye from the back seat.

I watched them drive away. The tears began to flow. I sat in my truck thinking I should hurry home and feed the boys, but the tears kept coming. A blurry red sun low in the sky hurt my eyes, but I deserved to be hurting. I deserved worse than bright light in my eyes. I deserved to experience terrible pain. I almost wished the spider had bitten *me*; but not quite, since I was fifteen years older than Alicia. Maybe too old to handle black widow bites.

It finally occurred to me that Solow, Boris and Willy shouldn't have to suffer just because I messed up. It was past their dinnertime. I drove away feeling like scum. Maybe I would feel better if I spent quality time with the boys, talking to Boris, romping with the goat, belly rubs for Solow. I felt tired just thinking about it. How could I possibly make up for my carelessness? I had almost killed my best friend...."

What's that red light for? I asked myself. *I'm not speeding.* I rechecked the rearview and noticed not only a motorcycle cop, but a long line of cars behind me. *Must be a funeral*, I thought, as I pulled off the road when the CHP officer bleeped his siren at me.

"Officer, I wasn't...oh, it's you."

"How's your friend doing?" His sunglasses reflected my image, red eyes, sad face—backlit by a red sun about to fall into the Pacific Ocean.

"She's going to be fine," I said. "Just has to go through a lot of paa...aain," I sobbed. I wiped my checks with the back of my hand.

"That's too bad. By the way, you need to speed up a little. You were holding up traffic."

"Oh, I was...sorry...sniff...and thanks for helping us today."

He gave my truck a pat with his gloved hand and went back to his motorcycle where he waited for me to continue on my way.

I drove the exact speed limit all the way to Prunedale, turned onto Langley Gulch Road and up the Trippys' long concrete driveway. The minute I stepped down from my seat, I heard Solow howling from the backyard.

Ma-ah, mah, mah accompanied him.

I almost smiled at the thought of the two playmates. I walked through the house and checked on Boris who sat on his perch, head under a wing.

I flipped the kitchen light on.

"What in Sam Hill?"

"Sorry, Boris, didn't mean to disturb you. Want a cracker?"

His top feathers stood at attention. "Boris wants a cracker."

I gave him a saltine, fresh water and a fresh bowl of seeds. He thanked me with a loud squawk, turned his back to me and adjusted his wings. Feeling rejected, I headed out the back door. The boys howled, bawled and bounced round and round my feet until I felt completely loved. Okay, they were hungry—I knew that. But still, they always gave me unconditional love, unlike a certain temperamental bird in the kitchen.

It seemed cruel to leave Willy outside alone, but the rules of civilization were constructed long before I had any say. I patted Willy on his little horns, scooped up poop from the sidewalk and apologized for leaving him alone.

Solow and I entered the kitchen.

"Back up! Back up now!"

"Take it easy, Boris. I'll fix you a cup of chamomile tea."

After I fed Solow his kibble, I grabbed a box of Oreos for myself and made a cup of hot chamomile tea. I sipped the first half of the soothing tea and saved the rest for Boris. When the tea had cooled to room temperature, I put the cup on the floor of his cage. He eyed me, cocking his head to one side.

"It's tea, Boris. Breana suggested I give it to you. Knock yourself out, I mean, help yourself."

Bad Boy Boris investigated the cup, circling it a couple of times. Finally, he poked his beak into Lois' china tea cup and scooped up the liquid with his bill until only a few drops remained.

Once the calming effects of chamomile tea quieted Boris and my chocolate binge kicked in, I relaxed. But thoughts of Alicia's suffering moved me to make a batch of mac and cheese from a box I found in the pantry.

After plenty of mac and cheese, I finally reached a high level of comfort-food saturation, feeling like an over-stuffed fifty-year-old with green eyes, wavy auburn hair and a large gut. I slugged my way across the kitchen to my purse and attended to messages from my cell phone and then Lois' answering machine. I leaned in closer and ran the last message again.

"Josephine, I need your help...." *Did I detect an accent?*

Chapter Five

Wednesday morning promised to be hectic. I began the day by calling my lanky friend, Kyle Larson, a nineteen-year-old art major at U.C. Santa Cruz. Kyle, Alicia and I had worked well together on large mural projects in the past. Early on, I had decided that the Crazy Horse project was not big enough for three painters getting in each other's way. But now that Alicia couldn't work, I needed to recruit Kyle. Naturally, he played hard-to-get, saying he had homework, a dentist appointment and an audition to play Hamlet in an up-coming U.C.S.C. Shakespearean production. I couldn't imagine him playing Hamlet with his red spiky hair, tattoos and multiple piercings. But I knew he would paint a fabulous herd of cows in the Wild West prairie painting at the Crazy Horse Saloon.

Kyle finally committed to painting Thursday, Friday and Saturday for starters. Because he needed money, he would rearrange parts of his schedule.

"So, Jo, is Alicia painting with us?"

"That's why I'm calling you, Kyle. Something happened to Allie yesterday, and she can't finish...actually it was my fault. I didn't bug-bomb my shed and a black widow spider hid in the pile of tarps...poor Allie was bitten...sniff." My lower lip trembled.

"Did she die?"

"Of course not, but her arm hurts a lot and she feels sick. And I feel sick about the whole thing."

"Yeah, like you probably feel really bad, like it was all your fault."

"Okay, Kyle, I said it was my fault. Gotta go. See you at the Crazy Horse Friday at ten." As I hung up the phone, I remembered the muffled message on Lois's machine. I played it three times and decided it had to be Breana speaking. I dug through Lois' kitchen drawers, found a little blue phone book of numbers and turned to *H*, the most likely place to find Henry, Henrietta and Hobblestone. I dialed the number but no one answered. I worked my brain, trying to remember Breana's last name. Was it Kennycott or Kinnicutt? Did it start with a K or a C?

I flipped through the little blue book and then the big phone book. No luck. Young people had cell phones only; and in my experience, they were usually not listed in an old-fashioned phone book.

I checked the clock on the microwave oven. It was eight-thirty. I had time for a quick breakfast and a trip down the hill to see if Henry's house was still standing. After that, I would be off to work and a trip to The Jewelry Company on Third Street in San Juan Bautista.

Too many things didn't add up at Henry's house. Who'd ransacked his place and why? Did Henry hide the ring in a sack of oatmeal before he/she died, and why would he do such a thing? Was the ring valuable? But the primary question was why did Henrietta pretend to be a guy? Her picture in the locket wasn't bad looking; and obviously, she had been married many years ago. Feeling pressed for time, I put my speculations aside until I had time to sort things out.

I fished the blue ring out of the sugar bowl and dropped it into my pocket.

Once the truck was loaded with work essentials, I drove down the Trippys' drive and up the Hobblestone driveway, pulling to a stop behind a Deputy Sheriff's car. I recognized Deputies Denise Lund, tall and blond, and Calvin Sayer, older, shorter and dark-complexioned. They approached my truck.

I climbed out of the driver's seat and greeted them with a "Good morning, officers."

"Mrs. Stuart, what are you doing here?" Lund asked in her usual flat tone.

"I'm house sitting up there." I pointed to the top of the hill. "At the Trippys' house. Last night I got a call from Breana Kinnicutt...."

"And you know Ms. Kinnicutt?" The officer cocked her head in a way that reminded me of Boris giving the evil eye.

"Of course, I know her. She wouldn't be calling a stranger."

"Mrs. Stuart...." Officer Sayer stepped closer, his manner warmer and kinder than Lund's by several degrees.

"You can call me *Ms.* I've been a widow for seventeen years."

"Sorry, *Ms.* Stuart, I just want to know what Ms. Kinnicutt was calling about."

"I wish I knew. It was a short message asking me to help her," I shrugged. "I would have tried to call her last night, but I was all messed up because my best friend got bitten by a spider and it was my fault...." A thought ran through my head. *If I admitted it was my fault enough times, would I eventually escape the dark feelings of guilt? I pictured myself as judge and jury pointing fingers at myself for the rest of my life.*

"Ms. Stuart," Officer Lund said, as Sayer pulled out a notebook and pencil, "did Breana sound like she was in danger?"

"Maybe...she sounded upset, but like I said, the recording was muffled. I have a question for you."

"Really?" She all but rolled her eyes.

"Did Breana report what happened to Henry's house the day before yesterday?"

"No, what happened?" Officer Lund held me hostage with her icy blue eyes.

"Well, some creep or creeps broke into Henry's house and tossed it. Breana and I cleaned up the mess."

"This happened when no one was home?"

I nodded and told them what the place looked like.

Officer Sayer asked if any doors or windows had been forced or broken.

"No," I said thoughtfully, trying to remember the whole shocking scene. "Breana would know for sure. I think you can find her at her apartment in Salinas or the college...."

"We checked there, Ms. Stuart," Officer Sayer said, handing me a card. "Call us right away if you hear from her."

I promised I would call.

They took off in a flurry of gravel and dust.

I waited until the cruiser was out of sight before I tried the doors. All locked. The screen on one window in the back looked beat up, like maybe someone had used it to crawl in and out of. I decided to see whether it was possible for a burglar to climb through the window. I pulled the screen off and jimmied the window frame upward. My leg wouldn't go up that high so I pushed a wheelbarrow against the wall, climbed onto it, leaned through the window and fell head first onto a bed. Unfortunately it didn't have a fat mattress like Lois' guest bed. I fell onto a skinny steel spring mattress that should have been junked fifty years ago.

I walked through the house rubbing the nape of my neck and right shoulder. The little house looked exactly as Breana and I had left it, except for one thing—a small pile of sorted mail. On the kitchen table next to the letters and advertisements was a torn corner piece of an envelope no bigger than a dime. I checked the wastebasket for the rest of the envelope, but it was empty.

Enough snooping, it was nine-thirty and I needed to go to work. I got in my truck and headed out. Prunedale to San Juan Bautista was a beautiful drive, windows down, music up. Golden hills waited for winter rains to make them green again.

I decided I had time to stop at the jewelers before checking in at the Crazy Horse. I parked in front of the Crazy Horse Saloon and walked one block south to The Jewelry Company. The little shop was locked up tight so I tried again on my lunch break. The door opened to the tinkle of a bell.

"Be right there," a tall gray-haired man said from across the room. He wore a jeweler's loupe contraption strapped around his head. Standing behind a high counter display of watches, he straightened up, turned off the humming tool in his hand and pulled off his loupe.

"I can come back later...."

"No, no, I'm coming." He sidled over to a lower counter. "What can I do for you?" He glanced at my Timex watch. "Need a battery?"

"No, my watch is fine, but I found this." I pulled the ring out of my pocket and placed it in the jeweler's hand. "And I'm wondering how much it's worth."

"How did you happen to find this ring?" he asked, flicking sugar granules out of the golden grooves with a fingernail.

"It's a long story, but in the end I found it in goat poop."

The man winced.

"Don't worry, I cleaned it," I smiled. "That's just sugar."

He turned the ring, looking at all sides from different angles. "It's pretty old, but I need time to examine the ring further before I can tell you anything about it. Fill out this form and come back Friday after five." He handed me a pen.

I filled the blanks with my name, phone number and address.

"Okay, I'll see you Friday." I handed over the paper and took the jeweler's business card from a display on the counter. David had recommended Mr. Samuel Rotsider, if ever I needed to replace my watch battery. I wasn't sure why he liked the man since the jeweler wasn't very personable and his assistant, a middle-aged woman wearing an outdated linen suit, nylons and thick-heeled shoes, hadn't said one word to me.

I walked slowly back to the Crazy Horse, mulling over Rotsider's shocked expression when he saw the ring. Two seconds later, he'd had no expression at all.

I walked into the restaurant. My eyes took a moment to adjust to the dim light as I rounded the bar. Below my bucking horse project was a giant collection of wine and liquor glasses. I made every effort not to touch or break them, but it was difficult to work in such tight quarters. The patrons were probably placing bets on whether I would break something.

I climbed my ladder holding a plastic cottage cheese container full of paint in one hand, a brush in the other. I leaned left and painted, leaned right and painted, moved the ladder a couple of feet to the right and applied another two feet of deep blue. While the paint was still wet, I grabbed a container of pale blue and blended it into the lower end of the deep blue with my two-inch brush.

Alonzo watched me balance while applying the eight-foot swath of sky. "How's your friend doing?"

"I haven't had a chance to talk to her today. She was pretty miserable yesterday." I made a mental note to call her later, as I blended in an even lighter blue, working it down to the horizon. By four-thirty, my interpretation of a western sky was finished, and I had added a far-away mesa along the horizon.

Alonzo would be opening up for happy hour soon, so I loaded everything into my truck and headed for Alicia's house in Watsonville.

Twenty-five minutes later, I parked in front of Alicia's lovely lake house. I took a moment to clear my head and paste a smile on my face.

I rang the doorbell.

Trigger opened the door.

"Hi, sweetheart, how's your mom today?"

"Daddy stayed home to take care of her. I don't know how she is, but she cries sometimes. I bring her things she wants, and I made a salad for dinner."

"May I come in and see her?"

"Sure, but Auntie Jo, be real quiet. I think she's asleep."

I followed Trigger to the living room, to a lump on the couch. It moved. A hand pulled back the blanket revealing Alicia's pale face and a tangled mass of shiny black hair.

"Hi, Jo," she groaned.

"Hi, Allie, can I get you anything? Where's Ernie?"

"He's taking a break." She pointed to a window overlooking the lake and a man sitting on the dock, feet in the water.

"Are you hurting…silly question…how can I help you?"

"Don't worry, Jo, I'll be all right…."

"I feel so bad, Allie. This was my fault. I should have bombed the shed. I'm so sorry this happened." I tried to keep it together, but tears were threatening.

I quickly walked to the kitchen and inspected Trigger's salad.

"Hey, Trigger, this salad looks delicious. What's the stuff on top...?"

"Fennel slices and chopped arugula and, see, that's a pear." He smiled. "Mom's been teaching me how to cook. After school I did everything she told me to do, and she always says, 'wash your hands with soap and don't cut your fingers.' "

"That's good advice. I'm glad you listen to your mother. Does she sit up, walk around at all?"

"Just to the bathroom, that's all." Trigger's smile faded.

I couldn't face Ernie. I told Trigger and Alicia I had to go home to feed the boys, which was true. Trigger said he would like to meet Boris and Willy someday. I promised to arrange it and left the house. I was such a coward, couldn't even be in the same room with my best friend.

At the last minute, I decided to stop at the grocery store since I was already in Watsonville. I knew I needed ice cream; the rest would come to me. Sure enough, I was able to find dozens of food items I couldn't live without.

My young friend Robert walked down the freezer aisle toward me proudly wearing his big blue apron and nametag.

"Hi, Robert."

"Jo, looks like you've cornered the comfort food department," he laughed.

"Yeah, having a bit of a hard time right now."

"That's too bad. Anything I can do?" His round freckled face turned serious.

"Yeah, you can undo the damage I caused. I almost killed my best friend."

"David or Alicia?"

"Alicia, but I don't want to talk about it."

"Hey, Jo, did you read in the paper about that dead guy who was really a woman…?"

"Yeah, what about it?"

"Forensics showed that the rifle had been wiped clean. How can someone shoot a gun and not leave prints? The victim wasn't wearing gloves."

"Wow, do they think it was murder?"

"What else?"

I drove home feeling overwhelmed with problems and unanswered questions. Should I spend my time worrying about Alicia, or Breana or the boys? Realistically, all I could handle was the care and feeding of the boys. I filled everyone's bowl—kibble for Solow, alfalfa for Willy and seeds for Boris.

I wasn't really hungry, just sad, so I scooped up a bowl of vanilla ice cream covered in chocolate syrup and caramel sauce with nuts and a dollop of whipped cream on top. Solow and Boris guilted me with sad eyes until I finally pushed away from the table and prepared a serving of ice cream for each of them and one for Willy.

"Boris wants a cracker."

"Don't complain, Boris, you have ice cream right there in front of that big honker of yours."

He dipped his bill into the ice cream. "Screech!"

"Try it—you'll like it."

Boris loved the ice cream once the shock of freezing cold food was over. The more he ate, the chattier he became. I made him a cup of chamomile tea as a chaser for the sugar-high.

"Boris is a baby." Squawk. "Where's wawa? Back up, now!" he chattered.

"Stuff it, Boris." I longed for peace and quiet.

"Hands up!"

I put my hands up and laughed at the ridiculous notion that Boris had any knowledge or control over what he said. Solow pushed against my knee. More guilt. Not enough time spent with Solow. I tried to remember when I gave him his last bath. Maybe when I had more time, we would swim in the pool. And then I remembered Willy. I turned on the patio lights and stepped outside. Solow pushed past me and romped on the grass with his goat buddy.

"Cock-a-doodle-doo!"

"What in the world...." I turned and looked up to the top of the pool shed. My jaw dropped. Solow and Willy paid no attention to a cocky little rooster on the roof. I suspected he'd flown in from Henry's place. He would have to help himself to bugs and worms because I was not about to go shopping for chicken food.

As if he could read my mind, the resplendent black and rust colored bird leaped down to the patio, marched into the shed like he owned it and pecked at Willy's food.

The phone rang. I hurried into the kitchen.

"Hello."

"Josie, I know it's kinda last minute, but I was wondering if you'd like some company this evening," David said.

"Actually, I would love some company, the human kind, that is. David, I'm going crazy around here. Every time I look around there's another critter needing food and attention. This evening, I was so tired I gave everyone ice cream. Solow and Willy are racing around the pool on a sugar high and Boris sounds like he's drunk, muttering obscenities. Maybe ice cream and chamomile tea don't go well together."

"Yeah, my kitty critters are pretty needy too, but they're all asleep right now. A good time for me to come see my sweetie. Did you say you gave them ice...never mind. I'll be right over."

David arrived twenty minutes later. We settled down on a plaid sofa in the den in front of the mega-screen TV and ignored it completely. It was a lovely evening until our conversation touched on a certain dead neighbor lady everyone thought was a man. David wanted to know what business it was of mine; and—if Henry was actually murdered—why didn't I just let the police find the murderer.

Of course, I wanted the police to find the murderer; but if I happened to come across relevant information, I would collect it and give it to the officers. Anyone would. And if I had to go a little out of my way to collect that information, well, *anyone* would.

"Anyone would be curious and want to help the police," I said.

"Not anyone, just *you*, Josie," he laughed, "just don't do anything dangerous."

Chapter Six

Thursday morning, lying in bed with my eyes closed, I thought about the quality time spent with David last night, and I never once told him about Alicia's spider bite and how guilty I felt. Maybe my guilt had taken a turn. Maybe it had stopped following me around, hanging on like a bad cold. There were other things I neglected to mention to David, like finding a mysterious gold ring and the fact that Henry's house had been tossed. David was a worrier and I hated to see him become overly exercised about every little thing in my life…still, I felt guilty for not telling him.

I opened one eye at the sound of *cock-a-doodle-doo*, stretched, checked the clock and quietly thanked the rooster for waiting until seven-thirty to mouth-off. Maybe he wasn't such a bad guy.

"Cock-a-doodle-doo!"

"I hear you, Roscoe," I grumbled as I tumbled out of bed, pulled on my robe and headed down the hall to Mr. Coffee, Solow at my heels. Boris sat quietly preening in the dim light. I decided Roscoe was as good a name as any for a mouthy little rooster. From a kitchen window, I looked for the boys—nowhere in sight. Actually, all I saw were faint outlines of patio furniture fading away into dense fog.

"No wonder Roscoe slept late."

"Boris wants a cracker."

"Yes, dear, coming right up," I snarked, and handed over a soda cracker. I filled Mr. Coffee, Solow's bowl,

Willy's bowl, came back to Boris and refilled his water dispenser.

"Boris, do you have any more pals coming to live with me?"

"Squawk!"

"I hope that was a *no*," I mumbled to myself, as I moved through the house to the front door. I picked up yesterday's soggy paper wedged between two gnomes, and a freshly thrown newspaper stuck in the branches of a large hydrangea.

Back in the kitchen, I set aside the sections of the paper I didn't care to read, poured a bowl of cereal for myself and leafed through the first four pages of the older paper. Page four featured an article laying out a theory that Henry did not shoot himself/herself. "There was not one fingerprint found on the gun, and Hobblestone was not wearing gloves when discovered by his housekeeper," the reporter wrote.

"It was murder, Boris."

"Squawk, put your hands up, now!"

"I think Boris needs a cup of tea." But the tea didn't happen. By the time I'd showered, dressed for work and spent a little time with the boys outside, I'd forgotten all about the tea. I grabbed my purse and set off for San Juan Bautista, ever grateful for the covered bed of my truck that worked so well as a storage unit for all my paints and equipment.

The fog thinned out as I turned left onto San Miguel Canyon Road and took the overpass onto Highway 101 North. A big sunny sky opened up ahead as I left Prunedale. My thoughts ran the gamut from worries about Alicia to excitement over the chance to paint some pretty nice art in a popular public place. I checked my fuel gauge—half a tank. I should have called Mom to let her know I was all settled in at the Trippys' house. My head whirled with things to do as I pulled to a stop in front of Alonzo's saloon.

Kyle's yellow Honda motorcycle roared up to my truck and skidded to a stop. He dismounted and walked up to me. He had a matching yellow helmet tucked under one arm, which he dropped in my truck bed for safekeeping. We filled our arms with paint equipment and entered the building.

I introduced Kyle to Alonzo and returned to the truck for a last load.

Kyle followed me outside. "I'll get that, Jo."

I pushed his hand away. "I got it. I'll take care of the tarps today."

"Oh, yeah, spiders." He turned and went back inside.

I shook each of the three tarps, spread them on the sidewalk and stomped them with my sandals. It was good therapy for me, but a couple of pedestrians coming my way turned and crossed the street. When I was certain no spider could possibly be alive, I folded the tarps and carried them inside.

Kyle and I went over the Wild West sketches. "I want people to feel the dust in the back of their throats when they look at this picture. You can lighten up on the number of cows. Just detail half a dozen and put the rest fading out in the dust."

"Cool."

Three hours later, Kyle had created a beautiful western sky with a few storm clouds and a flat horizon.

I had painted in the foreground of my painting— parched earth for the bucking horse to stand on. In the afternoon, I painted a beat-up old shed and a barn with a sign that read "Livery Stable."

Kyle brushed in his foreground, including the rocky dry gulch.

"Well, look at the time; let's pack up and go home," I said to Kyle, as we stood on the staircase for a better look at what we'd painted so far. "Wow, I feel a draft." I looked to the top of the stairs—nothing up there but a landing. I decided to check it out and climbed the stairs while Kyle loaded the truck.

The wooden stairs creaked and groaned all the way to the top where a gloomy hallway led to a small open window on the far wall; lace curtains swished and swayed to the rhythm of a playful breeze. Like the downstairs, the walls were dark wood with wide moldings and large beams overhead. I counted three doors on the right and three on the left. Five doors were numbered, but the first door on the right had *men* and *women* symbols on it. I peeked into the ladies' restroom which featured an old-fashioned four-legged bathtub and a tiny shower set-up.

"Hey, there, Josephine," Alonzo said, cheerfully, behind me.

"Oh, hi! Didn't hear you coming...I already used the downstairs restroom. Just wanted to see what this one was like. It's pretty cool...very retro."

"This one is for our tenants." He waved his hand at the five numbered rooms.

"Oh, I didn't realize you had renters in the building."

"That one across the hall is my office. I have room for one more tenant. My rates are pretty reasonable." He gave me a short history of the old hotel/saloon as we descended to the first floor. "I like what you two have painted so far," Alonzo said.

"Thanks; see you tomorrow." I slung a purse strap over my shoulder and walked to my truck, still smiling from the compliment given so early in the painting process.

Kyle waved and took off on his motorcycle.

I decided to take a short walk up the street to the jeweler to see if he'd had time to look at the ring. The door was locked and I didn't see anyone when I peered through the window. The last thing I noticed was a *closed* sign. Checking out the shop didn't feel like a waste of time, more like a therapeutic little walk in the fresh air.

Actually, the air smelled better than ordinary air. It had a flavor to it, like bakery goods, specifically, cinnamon rolls. Those rolls were calling my name. I stepped into the nearby bakery and bought a half dozen cinnamon rolls. I munched on one roll as I drove to Watsonville, making sure they were good enough for the Quintanas.

Alicia looked about the same as the day before. She was lying on the couch half asleep. An old *Magnum* rerun played on TV but she wasn't watching. I would have to be really, really sick to not watch *Magnum*.

I tried to make conversation, but she wasn't interested.

Trigger brought us tea but she didn't drink hers.

Ernie walked me out to the truck. "Thanks, Josephine, for the cinnamon rolls. Alicia hasn't been interested in eating anything all day. I guess it will take time. Doctor said it could be a month before the pain goes away."

"You're kidding…." I groaned.

"Don't worry, Josephine, Trigger likes to read to her and I do the cooking and cleaning. I'm on a leave-of-absence from the university."

I wished I had some words of comfort for Ernie, but I didn't. I motored home with no music, just guilt to keep me company. I filled the gas tank before leaving town. The sun was setting by the time I arrived at the Trippy house. The boys expressed their happiness with leaps and bleeps, barks, screeches and a boisterous cock-a-doodle-doo.

The all-boy chorus settled down as each bowl was filled and tummies were satisfied.

Finally, it was my turn to eat. After all my day's emotionally-charged, bad-eating choices, I went to work preparing a steak, baked potato and green salad dinner.

As I ate my food, Boris had his eye on a piece of potato skin that I'd pushed to the side of my plate. I carried my plate to the sink and handed him the potato skin. Boris took it with his beak and used his feet to pull it to pieces. He busily attacked the skin while Solow slept with his head on his food bowl. The boys outside had already settled down for the night. I cleaned the kitchen and called Mom and Dad.

"Oh, hi, Dad, sorry I didn't call sooner...."

"That's okay, honey, we just got back from Tahoe, did a little hiking while we were there. I'll get Leola for you." Mom and Dad typically hiked more on one trip than I did in a whole year. They lived in a nice little bungalow in Santa Cruz, and they were two candles short of eighty, but not ready to slow down.

"Hello, dear, I guess Bob told you about our trip to ride the rapids?"

"No, he said you went hiking."

"Yes, we did that too. If you can find the time, dear, you really ought to go white-water rafting—it's a hoot!"

I rolled my eyes. When would I ever be able to do such a thing? Life for me was work and more work. But I wasn't complaining. I loved my life, my friends and painting—except for those days when guilt had a chokehold on me.

"I'm taking care of the Trippys' house, like I told you. I agreed to take care of their cockatoo, but now I have a goat and a rooster as well."

"I know you'll do a wonderful job for the Trippys."

"Mom, you like genealogy, right? Can you look up something for me?"

"Certainly, we aren't going anywhere until next week."

"See if you can trace Henry Hobblestone, Henrietta Guthrie and Byron Guthrie. One or more of them might be from Houston, Texas, according to my friend, Breana."

"Yes, I saw the story about Henry being a female in the *Sentinel*. Remarkable. I'll work on it tomorrow, dear."

"Boris wants a cracker," Boris squawked.

"Thanks, Mom."

"Screech!"

"What was all that?"

"That's Boris, the cockatoo, wanting attention. Gotta go, Mom, love you." We hung up. I tried to imagine my folks staying home for the next three days—impossible.

Stepping outside with Solow at my feet, I decided it was time to kick back and enjoy the Trippys' palatial paradise of a backyard. My senses sprung to life with the scents of honeysuckle and mint planted in and around one of the gnome gardens, fresh-cut grass, thanks to landscapers Allen and Marvin, and chlorine fumes, thanks to the swimming pool. Brilliant stars spread out overhead, and my sweet boys wrestled and romped on the grass.

"What the…oh, yuck!" I stepped onto the lawn and dragged my shoe across the recently cut grass. Once my shoe was half decent, I located the broom and dustpan in the shed and deposited piles of goat poo in the garbage can. I finally settled back on a lounge chair but only for a moment.

The deep growl of a familiar sounding engine interrupted a chorus of crickets. My head snapped to the right toward a grand silhouette of coastal hills cutting Prunedale off from the Pacific Ocean. I followed the noise to the edge of the hill and looked down, but the second hill hid Henry's property from my view. All was quiet, but I felt responsible for Henry's house, so I loaded Solow into the truck, and we chugged over to the neighbors. I parked next to a black Harley.

I told Solow to stay quiet. As I turned to climb out of the truck, I was startled by a face in my window and a tiny flashlight pointed at my eyes.

"Sorry, Josephine. Didn't know it was you," Nate said, pointing the light away from my face. "Let me help yah down." He put out a gloved hand.

"Thanks, Nate, I'm just checking on the property...." I didn't move from my seat.

"Good thing, cause I saw someone leavin' just before you drove up."

"Did you see who it was?"

"'Fraid not; he raised a lotta dust leavin' here."

Solow growled softly.

"Quiet, Solow." I turned back to Nate. "Was it a car, truck, motorcycle?"

"Don't know, like I said, it's dark and he raised a lotta dust."

"I need to talk to Breana about something. Can you give me her cell phone number? And yours, while we're at it." Before he had time to answer, I opened my purse and pulled out two business cards and a pen. I handed them to the young man. "You keep a card for yourself and call me if you see anything suspicious going on here."

Nate scribbled two phone numbers on the back of a card and handed it back to me.

I fired up the truck, and Nate followed me on his motorcycle to Langley where he turned right and I turned left and left again up to the Trippy house. I instantly recognized Breana's compact Nissan parked in the spacious driveway. Solow and I approached her car which bore a Santa Cruz Derby Girls sticker on the back bumper.

Breana opened her car door. "Mercy, Josephine, I'm so glad you came home!" She twisted herself out of the driver's seat and looked around. "Might I be comin' in?"

I noticed the inside of her car was stuffed full of household items and clothes.

"Of course." I led the way.

Solow peed a ring around a happy gnome couple and caught up to us at the front door.

Once inside, we migrated to the kitchen, probably because the rest of the house was luxurious but not welcoming.

Boris looked up. "Squawk, hands up, now!"

"You silly ol' bird," Breana laughed.

"Silly bird…Boris wants a cracker."

I quickly fetched one just to keep him quiet, and put on the tea kettle.

"Have you eaten dinner?" I checked the clock—nine-thirty.

"Not really…."

I pawed through the fridge for *easy meal* ideas.

"Would you like a steak sandwich?"

"You don't have to do that, Josephine…."

But I already had the meal figured out, a steak sandwich with a little coleslaw on the side, no problem.

Breana ate her meal while Boris chattered and Solow watched for any food that might fall his way.

I made a cup of tea for Boris and, minutes later, the boys were asleep.

"Breana, I got your phone message, but I couldn't get back to you. I didn't have a number." I held up the card Nate had written their phone numbers on. "But I have one now. What's going on?"

"Last night I decided to stay at Henry's because my apartment smelled of fresh paint. He went ahead and painted my place—the landlord did—before I moved out, the old fool. I thought I'd spend the night at Henry's; but when I drove up to the house, I saw someone walking across the yard toward the front of the house. He had a torch in his hand."

My jaw dropped. "A torch? Like with fire?"

"Sorry, I mean a flashlight. I was scared so I squealed my car round the tree and down the drive. At the bottom of the hill, I pulled onto the shoulder and called you; but I saw headlights in my rear windscreen and sped down to the freeway. I was so unnerved I raced all the way back to my smelly apartment, still shaking, I was."

"That's too bad. Any idea who was after you?"

"About that, I really don't know. I came here tonight because I don't know where else to go." She looked at the ceiling for a moment as if the answer to her problems might be written there. "The landlord put my things out—right there on the sidewalk while I was attending my nursing class today. I was so embarrassed to find my belongin's laid out for everyone's eyes to see."

"Actually, Breana, I just happen to know where you can rent a room for a reasonable price. Alonzo showed it to me at the Crazy Horse Saloon."

"It's a bit late…."

"You can stay here tonight. Don't worry about a thing. Tomorrow, we'll get you settled at the Crazy

Horse." Even as I spoke, I wondered if Breana would bring trouble to the Trippy house. What if someone was stalking her? Did she have enough rent money to live at the Crazy Horse? Why did my mouth always precede my brain?

"Excuse me a minute, I need to call Lois," I said, moving away from the table. I watched Breana tearing into her sandwich, devouring every crumb.

I dialed Lois' cell number. It rang a dozen or more times. "Hallow?"

"Hi, Lois; it's me, Josephine Stuart...."

"Oh, Gawd! Hello, Josephine," she said.

I heard snoring in the background. "We have a situation here...."

"So do *we*, Josephine. It's four o'clock in the morning here in Madrid."

"Sorry, Lois, but I need to know if Henry had any relatives who might be poking around in his house. And if there are any, what might they be looking for. Did he have a will?"

"I don't know about a will. The only relative he ever spoke about was a grand niece living in Texas, Houston, I believe. I don't know her full name. He called her Elvira, said she was a big gal who worked in construction her whole life. Is that all?" she yawned.

"Yeah, thanks, Lois. Sleep tight." We hung up. I would have asked a few more questions and maybe told her about the four extra guests staying in her house, but at four in the morning her brain was anything but lucid. I looked over at Breana's empty plate, her slumped shoulders and eyes at half mast.

"Hey, Breana, let's get your PJs out of your car. You can have the blue room down the hall from me. It's real pretty if you like floral prints on everything. And you have a bathroom to match."

When we were finally settled in our bedrooms, lights out, I said good night to Breana.

She said, "Good night, Josephine. Did I tell you that Henry's address book is missing?"

My eyes popped open.

Chapter Seven

My favorite day of the week finally arrived with a cock-a-doodle-do from the backyard followed by a bad imitation from the kitchen. Friday would not be the last day of the work week for me, but most Fridays meant dinner at Alicia's. Then I realized *that* probably wouldn't happen for a while since my friend was so sick. I made a mental note to call Alicia as I rolled out of bed. I looked at Solow's empty bed and heard the shower down the hall. Oh, yeah, Breana—my next project.

All showered and dressed, Breana and I split up the breakfast chores. Solow ate the scraps and Boris sipped a cup of tea.

"I wuv you," the big bird crooned.

"That's so sweet. I wuv you too, Boris," I said.

"Squawk!"

"We always say that to one another," Breana smiled.

"Oh, I thought…never mind. I'm getting used to him. Does Lois get along with Boris?"

"Pretty well, she does. She doesn't like cuddly things like cats and dogs."

"Breana, you said something last night, or did I dream it? Something about an address book…."

"Yes, I thought it peculiar that it turned up missin'. I wanted to get a hol' of Henry's niece. Surely her information would be in the little blue book on the bookshelf; but when I looked, it was gone; would you believe that?"

"When did you look for it?"

"Tuesday, I believe, the day after the house was torn apart and you helped me clean it all up. Maybe that was the very thing the thieves were after, do you think?"

We decided to check out Henry's place once all the critters were fed.

Breana spent some time chatting with Boris while I checked on Solow, Willy and the rooster. Roscoe seemed to be doing fine on goat food. If only I could potty-train them. It crossed my mind that Solow's ancestors were bird dogs. Did he know that the rooster was a bird? And then I remembered that Roscoe had all the machismo and Solow was sweetness and light. I could trust him.

I drove down to Henry's and Breana followed in her car. We parked next to a dusty white Ford 350 pickup truck with Texas plates. We both had keys to the front door. Anxiously, I stood back as she used her key. The door creaked open.

"Oh, my God!" Breana whispered and stepped back.

I squeezed around her and poked my head in the door. A large middle-aged woman sat in Henry's favorite chair, head back, mouth open. A lap blanket covered her legs, but not her massive sandaled feet. She had a rhythm going as she puffed and snorted, puffed and snorted.

Breana froze at the front door.

I moved cautiously toward the leathery-skinned, black-haired, no-frills woman.

Breana came up to me and whispered, "She looks a bit like Henry. She might be his...."

"Snort, snort, gasp." The woman's eyes blinked open and rolled in our direction. She sat up straight, reached into the breast pocket of her denim shirt and handed me a piece of folded paper. "It's from the coroner."

I unfolded the paper and glanced at it. "So you're a relative....?" I said.

"Yep, the only one left—only one I know of, anyway. That's me—Elvira Guthrie—Henry's niece. I'm the whole family tree standin' right here before ya. When I found out Uncle Henry was dead, I decided to come see what he left me." She looked around the rustic room, her face weathered, eyes wrinkled, lips smiling.

"You drove all the way from Texas?" Breana asked.

"Oh, sure; planes don't bother me, but I like to drive—saves money that way. People think all Texans are rich. I work hard for a livin'—no oil in my portfolio." Elvira produced a husky laugh ending in a snort as she stood up to her full six feet, two hundred pounds.

"Well, ah, this is Breana, Henry's housekeeper, and I'm Josephine...I'm house-sitting up the hill. I'm sort of in charge of the property until things get sorted out."

"I hope it's okay that I made myself at home," she said.

I noticed a black suitcase in front of the bedroom door.

"Don't worry, Josephine," Breana said, "I'll be happy to be stayin' at the Crazy Horse."

I told Elvira we would visit her after work.

She walked us to the door.

As we drove away in our separate vehicles, I wondered if I should have warned Elvira about burglars and such. In the end, I decided she could easily take care of herself. The road to San Juan Batista was a breeze—no traffic except for Breana following me. I curbed the truck behind Kyle's motorcycle and waited by the door for Breana. She parked, joined me and together we entered the Crazy Horse.

We found Kyle at the bar sipping a tall lemonade. "Jo, there's been a change. Alonzo wants to, like, replace the Father Serra idea with this one." He pointed to the open book of famous western paintings on the bar.

"A dance hall girl and a poker game?"

"Yeah, he said people complained that the old picture was gone so we gotta paint a new one." He glanced at Breana.

"Fine, we'll deal with that later. Kyle, this is my friend Breana."

"Nice to meet you," he said, his face flushing like a schoolgirl.

"Let's get our stuff out of the truck. I'll carry the tarps. Where's Alonzo?"

"He's up there," Kyle pointed.

"Breana, just go up those stairs and knock on the first door on the left."

She hesitated for a second, put her shoulders back and climbed the stairs.

"Kyle and I hustled everything into the restaurant and began another day of painting. My job was to create an old western desert town as a background for the up-close bucking horse. I had to create a four-foot by eight-foot horizontal painting taken from a photograph of a famous painting with a vertical format and very little background. I flipped through the book, gathering ideas for buildings and cacti from other paintings, ignoring stares from two old coots at the bar.

Half an hour later, Breana and Alonzo clomped down the ancient wooden staircase, talking and laughing.

Alonzo, looking good in a western shirt, Levis and boots, greeted me. "We have a new tenant at the Crazy

Horse," he smiled. "I'm going to show Ms. Kinnicutt the town, get some fresh air and all."

I watched them leave the building. Their laughter faded as they walked south on the patchwork sidewalk and then crossed the street. Alonzo was a head taller than Breana. Her hair glistened in the bright sunlight. Some might envy their youth, but I would not have wanted to be young again. I actually liked being fifty.

The geezers toddled out the door, high on lattés and war stories.

Kyle and I were alone except for Daisy, a young waitress who bustled around, setting tables for the lunch crowd. My concentration improved and I was able to lay in some cacti and a water tower. Kyle painted two distant cows—the beginning of the herd. We barely noticed Breana and Alonzo as they wandered back into the building an hour later, still chatting and laughing like long-time friends.

Breana said goodbye to everyone and left for her nursing class in Salinas.

Alonzo mixed drinks for two older women having lunch at a table by the front window. The lunch clientèle was light—half a dozen tables, but I'd heard that the Crazy Horse enjoyed a very good dinner business.

Kyle and I took a lunch break and ordered sandwiches. Daisy gave us free soft drinks with our order. I ate fast, paid the bill and left Kyle at the table eating his BLT and half of mine.

I hurried down the street to The Jewelry Company and opened the door a crack. The bell tinkled.

Mr. Rotsider looked up from his work. "Five o'clock," he grumped.

Did I appear to be too eager? It wasn't like Rotsider had crowds of customers. He was old enough to retire and probably set in his ways. I closed the door, walked north one block and joined Kyle who was still eating. It was two in the afternoon, and many of the lunchers were leaving or had already left.

An overhead fan churned out a bit of cool air.

I called Alicia. She answered in person.

Feeling excited and hopeful, I asked how she felt.

"Not too bad," she said, "Ernie took me to the doctor today because my bite was infected."

"Oh, no, really?" I gasped, as guilt ran through my veins.

"I'm taking antibiotics. It will be better soon," she sighed.

"I was hoping you were much better...."

"It will take time, be patient, Jo."

"I'll try. It's just that I feel so bad for you...."

"You didn't know this would happen. Relax. You can bring me a box of chocolates if that will make you feel better. You know the ones I like."

"Okay, see you around six."

"Ernie's making albondigas soup for dinner. Guess you'll have to stay and help us eat it," she chuckled. We hung up.

Kyle finished eating and we went back to painting. I let him go home at four-thirty, but I stayed a little longer. I needed to see my painting from another angle so I crossed the dining room and climbed halfway up the stairs. As I turned to look down on my painting, I thought I heard a whisper. A cool breeze ruffled my hair. I looked over my shoulder—no one there. Goosebumps broke out as I fled the staircase. I went back to my painting feeling foolish.

"Josephine, you look like you've seen a ghost," Alonzo laughed, as he towel-dried one wine glass, then another.

"You tell me...what's up there?" I asked, still feeling creeped-out.

"A ghost, of course, and perfectly harmless."

"Well, that's not the answer I wanted to hear. Did you tell Breana about Ms. Ghost?"

"Sure. She took it pretty well—after all, the Irish believe in the little people." He set the towel aside.

I rolled my eyes. "It's almost five o'clock so I'm going to load up the truck and go."

"I'll help you," Alonzo said as he folded Kyle's ladder.

"Thanks, Alonzo, but the ladders go in last." Once we had loaded everything into the truck bed, I pulled the top down.

Alonzo went back inside.

I checked my watch—five-oh-five, time to see the jeweler. I marched down the block. The bell tinkled as I walked into the jewelry store and looked around.

"Ms. Stuart, your ring has been cleaned." Rotsider came out from behind the counter and handed me a very small clear plastic bag with the ring inside.

"Wow, it looks beautiful." I held it up to the light.

"This ring is an old Bezel-style hinged ring with a sapphire stone from the Renaissance period."

"A sapphire stone…." I choked. "This big?"

"The ring is genuine, but the stone is glass. Not the real thing." He handed me a bill for twenty-five dollars.

I paid the bill, stuffed the ring into my breast pocket and thanked Mr. Rotsider. A rush of feelings had me excited, confused and deeply disappointed all at the same time. Had there been a real sapphire on the ring, originally? If so, how did it happen that the sapphire had been replaced with glass?

I walked to my truck thinking, why should I care? It wasn't my ring. I would have to wait to find out who the heir was. Elvira was a pretty good bet, and the ring would probably fit at least one of her chunky fingers.

I turned the key and motored up Highway 129 toward Watsonville. On my way to the Quintana house, I stopped at the grocery store to pick up wine, candy and flowers. I carried everything in my arms and placed it all on the counter of Robert's check stand.

"Feeling guilty about something?" he laughed.

"Yeah, how did you know? Did I tell you about the spider?"

"Huh? Refresh my memory." Robert scratched his head.

"The black widow that bit Alicia...never mind, just ring me up." I checked my watch. Alicia was expecting me to arrive at her house an hour ago.

"I can carry this out for you, Josephine."

"Thanks, Robert, but I'm in a hurry." I dashed out the door with my cache of goodies, fired up the truck and minutes later parked in front of Alicia's house.

The Quintanas were as welcoming as ever. Homemade Mexican soup and Trigger's specialty salad felt like a warm blanket on a cold night. As usual, Alicia and her family comforted me even though I went there to help her.

"Allie, you're looking better."

"Amazing what a shower can do," she laughed, as she awkwardly dipped a spoon into her soup bowl using her left hand because her right arm was in a sling.

"Mom takes naps all day, and I tie her shoes for her," Trigger said.

"You're the greatest, Trigger! And I love the salad you made. Have you ever seen one of these?" I asked, pulling the ring out of my pocket.

Trigger's eyes went big as he held the bagged ring.

"You can take it out of the bag...."

"Is this for David?" he asked.

"No, it's not mine to give to anyone. I'm just holding it until I find out who will inherit it. It's really not a big deal anyway. It's not real."

Ernie asked to see the ring and Trigger handed it to him. He felt it, turned it and held it to the light. "This looks like the real deal, a ring from the Renaissance period."

"Yeah, but the top is glass."

"I'm wondering why they'd use glass for something like this. These rings were for the wealthy. They used real gemstones like emeralds, diamonds and sapphires." He passed the ring back to me. "I know someone who'd love to take a look at this thing. He has Pacific Avenue Jewelers. Louden's a real history buff."

"I just might do that, but right now I have to run. My boys are hungry, all four of them."

"Four?" Alicia groaned.

"I now have a rooster to take care of." I stood up and thanked them for a wonderful meal. We hugged and I left the warm blanket of Watsonville for the needy boys of Prunedale. But my greeting at the Trippy house was warm and sweet in its own way. I dropped the ring into the sugar bowl and took care of Roscoe and Willy first.

I didn't turn on the outdoor lights, preferring to enjoy dusk and cricket songs under a full moon.

When the goat and rooster had been fed, Solow followed me into the kitchen for a bowl of kibble and fresh water.

"Boris wants a cracker."

"Hold your horses, old boy," I laughed. Boris needed fresh food, water and newspaper in his cage. As I bent down to lay out the newspapers, he jumped down from his perch onto my shoulder, startling me. I tried to be calm, as if a large bird walking across my shoulder was no big deal. He gently pecked at my ear. But what if he suddenly went into one of his moods, would he rip off my ear?

I slowly backed out of the cage. When I stood up straight, Boris was still on my shoulder, his talons clinging to my shirt. I began moving about the kitchen, pretending not to care if there was a big bird on my shoulder nibbling at my hair with his beak. I made him a cup of chamomile tea, leaned into the cage and placed the teacup on the fresh newspaper. Boris strolled down my arm and dipped his nose into the fresh brew. I was finally able to back out of the cage and close the door.

Boris heard the door fastener and looked up from his tea. "Squawk!"

"Take it easy, old boy; it's bedtime for you."

Solow looked up from his nap, recognizing the *bedtime* word.

"Take it easy, Solow. I'm tired too, but first we're going for a little ride down to Henry's place."

He responded to the *ride* word and beat me to the front door.

As I drove up to the little house and cut the engine, the porch light blinked on. The front door swung open. Most of the light from inside was blocked by a large figure in the doorway.

"Howdy, Josephine! I knew you'd get here sooner or later. Who's that ya got there?"

"Hi, Elvira, this is Solow. We stopped by to see if you need anything."

"Come on in." She motioned for me to sit down. "I found enough food in the freezer to make it through today, but I'll have to shop tomorrow."

"Sounds like you're doing okay. Did the coroner write to you about the strange thing about Henry?"

Elvira laughed. "I've known it wasn't Henry for twenty-two years. See, he came to Texas to his sister's house—my grandmother—for a visit. Grandma called me as soon as he arrived. Said he didn't look good. She asked me to come over and help her take care of him. I didn't know what she was talking about, but I jumped in my truck and high-tailed it thirty miles to her house in the middle of the night. Grandma calls, you go!" Elvira paused to look at her thumbnail.

"So why did your grandma call you?" I was on the edge of my seat.

"I walked in and there's Uncle Henry stretched out on the floor, dead as a daffodil in Jooly. Grandma was widowed and never liked Texas, so she saw the whole thing as a way for her to get to California. All she had to do was cut her hair real short and wear her brother's clothes. I thought she was a bit loony, but I helped her anyway. I was thinkin' she wouldn't really go through with the idea."

"What did you do with Henry?"

"Oh, he's in a nice shady place under a blue wood tree in Grandma's backyard."

"Let me get this straight, your Grandma was Henrietta, Byron Guthrie's widow."

"Right, and she came to California with Henry's identification, wearing his clothes. Lucky for her that they were close in size and looks except her butt was bigger, but I guess nobody around here noticed."

"Did she wear Henry's watch, rings and things like that?"

"Everything he came with she took on as hers. I still think it's the funniest thing I ever heard of, but I went along with it for Grandma's sake. I just hope I don't lose *my* brain when I get to her age," she laughed.

"Did you ever come out here for a visit?"

"Just once, six years ago. Glad I got to see her before she passed. Seemed like after a while, she actually believed she was Henry, she played the part so well."

"Elvira, are you expecting a big inheritance?"

"Don't you think that's a little personal, Josephine?" Her easy smile disappeared. I just got here and you want to know if Grandma was loaded...."

"Sorry, not my business, but I am interested in finding out who murdered your Grandma."

Elvira's jaw dropped. "Murdered?"

I wondered if she was truly shocked or just play-acting, seeing as how acting ran in the family.

Chapter Eight

I called Alicia Saturday morning to see how she was feeling. She said she still couldn't raise her arm, but she felt good enough to do a little reading. She Googled the town of San Juan Batista and read a few of the articles to me, noting that the Crazy Horse Saloon had been built on a lot where the town hanging tree had been located. Near the tree, in the 1800s, a Mexican man had shot Manuel Butron, who suffered from epileptic fits. Manuel was shot through his chest, survived and never had another epileptic fit. However, the man who shot Manuel was hung from the infamous willow tree.

"What an interesting history," I said.

"That's nothing; the whole town is haunted and there's a tunnel that goes from the Crazy Horse up to the mission."

"Wow, that's a long tunnel; the mission is several blocks away. I'm glad you're feeling better, Allie. I have to run now—Saturday's a workday. Talk to you soon." We hung up.

I dialed Lois Trippy.

"Hello," Lois yawned.

"Hi, Lois, it's Josephine." Before she could complain about the late hour, I quickly asked my question. "Lois, when you were looking up Henry's family on the Internet, did you find any other living relatives beside Henrietta and her granddaughter, Elvira?"

"Yawn...I'll call you tomorrow. We just got in from an exhausting tour."

I finished eating my breakfast, checked to see that all my boys had food and water and drove to my home in Aromas. As I motored up Otis Road, I felt like I wanted to stay. I loved the neighborhood, but I only had time to pick up the mail, water the marigolds and check my answering machine. I made a mental note to call Mom later.

I rushed through my chores, said a silent goodbye to my sweet little house and cruised slowly down Otis, but only for a short minute. David stood at the end of his driveway waiting for me. I braked. He circled the truck and leaned in the window for a kiss. The rest of my trip to San Juan Bautista was filled with warm, tingly thoughts of David.

I curbed the truck in front of the Crazy Horse.

Kyle came up to my window. "Like, what's with the big smile, Jo?"

"Nothing, just thinking." My cheeks burned. "Let's unload the truck."

Alonzo greeted us as we walked into the grandiose dining room. I carried my ladder under one arm, eyes straining in the dim light. When I turned to my right to ask where Breana was, my ladder swung to the left whacking Breana below her knees.

"Breana, are you okay? I'm so sorry...I didn't see you there."

"Saints be praised! Nothin's broken, Josephine. Don't you worry now," she grimaced.

"Maybe a little walk will do you good?" Alonzo said.

"Maybe it would at that," she chirped, pirouetting and stepping out the door with the young restaurant owner.

My cell phone rang.

I leaned the ladder against table legs and dug through my purse for the phone. It was Mom. She said she'd been able to trace Henry's family back to Captain Stone, an infamous pirate in the late 1700s who made his living robbing Spanish and French merchant vessels in the West Indies. He began his sailing career with Blackbeard and eventually acquired a ship of his own. In the 1800s, his great grandchildren were forced to give their inherited booty back to the Spanish government.

I thanked Mom for her work and hung up the phone. All I could think about for the rest of the day was the ring Willy had delivered to Lois' patio, the ring still in my possession. I suddenly needed a second opinion.

While Kyle painted his assigned masterpiece, I stepped outside and down the block to the jeweler's shop. I tried the door, cupped my hands against the window glass and peered into the dark room. Is no one around at eleven o'clock in the morning on a Saturday? "Saturday! Shoot, I forgot it was Saturday," I scolded myself.

I pulled away from the window when I saw a handsome young couple reflected in the glass. They crossed the street and asked what I was looking for.

"Nothing, really, just wanted to stretch my legs," I said to Breana.

"Old Rotsider's getting closer to retirement," Alonzo said. "Opens his shop when he feels like it."

"Do you think he will open it today?"

"He might…time for me to get back to work." Alonzo excused himself and walked quickly up the sidewalk.

Breana and I took our time getting back to the Crazy Horse, chit chatting as we walked.

"How did you meet Nate?" I asked.

Breana looked startled as she yanked her happy thoughts away from Alonzo, and over to Nate. "One day I was cleanin' house for Henry, and I answered the door. There was Nate wantin' to talk to Henry about a job. Henry looked confused when Nate said he'd talked to the old man on the phone. Henry didn't remember talkin' to Nate on the phone, but he said he'd pay to have some fallen limbs chopped into firewood. Nate set about to do a good job for Henry, and I carried some water to him. It was a foggy day in June, but sweaty he was, throwin' off his jacket."

"So you met him a year ago?"

"No, it was this last June. We really don't know each other that well…three months is all," she blushed.

"No serious strings?"

"Oh, no, just friends, we are."

We entered the Crazy Horse and Breana marched up the stairs to her room.

I painted until four-thirty and called it a day.

Kyle helped me pack up the truck and promised to be back to work Tuesday.

I drove to the Trippys' house, fed the boys and cleaned myself up for a date with David. Mom had invited us over for dinner. I slipped into my favorite fitted, button-down, baby-blue top with Navy blue slacks and matching sandals. I ran a brush through my hair, grabbed my purse and dashed to the front door, pausing a moment to look calm.

The doorbell rang a second time. I opened the door.

"Hey, beautiful…." He leaned down and kissed my cheek.

I locked the door behind us and we roared down the driveway in David's Jeep. Forty-five minutes later, we left the freeway and wound our way through Santa Cruz to an old but well-maintained neighborhood. Modest, old Victorian-style homes on small lots lined Walnut

Avenue, each with a tiny lawn neatly framed in foliage and flowers.

David parked at the curb and dashed around the Jeep to help me out.

"Aren't you the gentleman tonight," I teased, already halfway out of my seat.

"You looked a little tired so I thought I'd help you...."

"Yoo hoo, David, I need some help."

He stopped and turned to say hello to Mom as she walked down the sidewalk, her long silver earrings swinging.

"Bob's trying to burn down the neighborhood," Mom laughed as she grabbed David's arm and walked him to the front door. I caught up to them at the back door as they watched Dad flipping burgers and chicken legs on the BBQ amongst a gush of flames. He loved the excitement of a good barbeque.

It was seven-thirty, the sun hung low in the western sky and a barely visible moon rose up from the east.

David and I each carried a platter of blackened meat into the kitchen.

Mom pointed to a stack of plates and ordered us to try the kale and radish salad and a quinoa, arugula, apple and sausage salad she'd made for the first time. For me, the salads were scarier than out-of-control BBQ flames. I carried a pack of Tums in my purse for those times when my mother felt like reinventing traditional foods that were already perfectly good.

We settled into our chairs at the dining room table and cleaned our plates, almost. I washed pieces of kale off my teeth with a cup of freshly brewed coffee, and slipped a Tums lozenge between my lips when no one was looking.

David squirmed in his seat, but his color wasn't too bad.

Mom served her homemade banana bread with ice cream on the side.

I noticed David's eyes were watering so I slipped him a Tums.

"What are we celebrating?" I asked.

"Bob's bowling team won the Tri-County Tournament," she beamed.

"It was nothing, any great athlete could have done what I did," he said as he stood up and took a bow. "While I'm up, more coffee anyone?"

"Not for me, thank you. I don't want to spoil my nap on the way home."

"Still falls asleep in the car like a little girl," David laughed.

"Mom, did you find out any more about Captain Stone?"

"No, but I looked for other relatives and I think Henry's niece had a baby boy, although there's no record of her being married. Henry had a sister, Henrietta, but there's no record of her death so I assume she's alive somewhere. She would be close to one-hundred years old...." Mom shrugged.

"Remember I told you that Henry was a she?"

"Yes and I read it in the paper. What are you getting at, dear?"

"Henry's sister, Henrietta buried her brother in Texas and came to California pretending to *be* her brother. She got away with it too. It looks like Elvira is her granddaughter and will inherit everything. If only we could find a will and make sure. And a will might point to the murderer."

"I thought Mr. Hobblestone was accidentally killed when he was cleaning his own gun," Mom said.

"That's what the paper said originally, but later forensics proved he didn't shoot himself. There were no prints on the gun. It had been wiped clean. I still think a will might be helpful."

David rubbed his chin. "If there's a will, it would probably be on record with an attorney. I'll ask my old friend Stilts if he knows anything."

"Who's Stilts?" I asked.

"He's a retired lawyer. He lives in Aromas."

"Mom, do you think you can find more information on Elvira? The Hobblestones are an odd bunch, and I want to make sure she is who she says she is."

"I'll try, dear," Mom yawned. "Sorry, long day lawn bowling and then kayaking in the lagoon."

Bob nodded his sunburned head.

"We should be going," I said, pushing back my chair.

David shook Dad's hand, kissed Mom on her cheek and walked me to his Jeep. The ocean air and starry sky sparked my romantic side. I watched David's handsome profile as he maneuvered through Santa Cruz traffic and finally merged into the southbound flow on Highway One.

"Josie, I'll contact Stilts Monday. Is there anything else I can do to help?"

"There is one thing. Would you mind taking the ring to Ernie's jeweler in Watsonville?"

"No problem. This is kind of fun."

"Wow, David, I never thought you would get interested in solving a mystery." But I was glad to see him interested instead of trying to steer me away from such things—more fuel for my romantic furnace.

David parked in front of the Trippys' house and helped me down from my seat. We walked arm-in-arm to the front door. I inserted the key, but it only locked the door. After a few tries, I realized the door had been unlocked in the first place. But I remembered locking it when we left.

"Josie, you're shivering."

"Yeah, something's not right," I said as I pushed the door open. I flipped a light switch and gasped. Solow galloped up to me looking guilty of something, but I knew it wasn't Solow who'd torn the place apart. Willy leaped over a spotless mauve sofa and bounced into the dining room where he'd knocked over a Tiffany lamp and the small table supporting it.

"What in the world happened here?" David muttered.

"Lois isn't going to like this. Help me catch Willy," I shouted over my shoulder as I took off after the little goat. He seemed to think it was all a game, hopping onto the kitchen table and jumping off the other side, scrambling under it and then over the top again while Boris screeched and flapped his wings. We eventually cornered Mr. Frisky in the kitchen. I grabbed his collar and unceremoniously hauled him out the back door.

"If you weren't so cute, I'd kick your little fanny," I said, and slammed the door. "It really isn't Willy's fault."

"Obviously, someone let him in the house. Who do you think it could be? Were those drawers open when you left the house?" He pointed to three kitchen drawers half open.

"Nope! Someone's looking for the ring."

"How do you know that?" he asked as I reached for the sugar bowl.

"What else could it be?" I dug into the sugar with two fingers, felt the ring and pulled my fingers out of the bowl. "At least the ring is safe. Let's check out the rest of the house."

"Boris wants a cracker."

"Not now, old boy," David said. "Does he need food?"

"No, his bowl is full."

Boris sidled across his perch. "Hands up, now! Squawk."

We ignored his antics and examined every room, every closet. The kitchen, den and my bedroom had been thoroughly tossed and searched. The rest of the house seemed untouched except where Willy had romped and chewed.

I stood staring at my room. Someone had emptied my suitcase, leaving my underwear strewn across the carpet. My bathroom looked like Hurricane Hilda had passed through it. The hairs on the back of my neck stood at attention when I saw my hairdryer in the toilet.

"That's it, I'm calling 911," I groaned.

"Of course, we will," David said, pulling his phone out of his pocket.

David made the call while I went back to the kitchen to try and clear my head. First Henry's house is searched, now it was the Trippys' house. In both cases, the lock was picked. The ring was the only common denominator, but I wasn't ready to tell the authorities about its existence yet. They could help themselves to fingerprints and question me all night long, but I decided not to tell them everything yet.

Lucky for me, officers Sayer and Lund didn't ask those kinds of questions. They dusted the front door for prints and asked if I knew who did it? Duh! Of course, I didn't know who did it. Am I a mind reader?

Five minutes after the sheriff's cruiser disappeared down the driveway, I was calling Lois, hoping she could shed some light on the house sitting nightmare I found myself in.

"Josephine, it's six in the morning in Rome...." Lois yawned.

"I'm sorry, Lois, but your house was broken into and ransacked...."

"What? You don't mean it…tell me what happened. Tom, wake up!" Her voice went from soft to shrill in two seconds.

"I thought maybe you could tell me why someone would break in. They left the goat in the house…."

"What goat?" she screamed.

"Henry's little goat, Willy. His manners are just fine outdoors, but he's pretty destructive inside the house."

"Josephine, get that goat out of my house!"

"He's outside with Roscoe…."

"Who's Roscoe?"

"Henry's rooster. He shares the pool house with Willy."

"We'll be home in twenty-two days. I hope things will be back to normal by that time," she growled.

"Did I tell you that Henry's niece, Elvira, is in town?"

"I knew that. She identified the body. I'll talk to you later when I calm down."

Lois hung up.

"Wow, that's curious," I said.

"What, Josie?"

"Lois just told me that Elvira identified Henry/Henrietta's body."

"Yeah, what about it?"

"Henry died thirteen days ago."

"Yeah…?"

"Elvira told *me* she just arrived in California yesterday."

Chapter Nine

Sunday morning, I stumbled down the hall following the scent of freshly brewed coffee. David laid the newspaper down on the kitchen table, took a last sip of coffee and told me he had to get back to his kittens. He hadn't planned to be gone so long. Last night, my gentleman friend told me he couldn't leave me alone after the break-in. David had been a great comfort to me. But as the sun came up, my fears melted away.

David and I had straightened up the Trippys' house after the deputies left. We worked until midnight, but the place needed more than just putting books back on shelves and filling drawers and cupboards. Willy had knocked over a potted cactus and Solow's water bowl, leaving a trail of muddy footprints all over the living room and dining room carpet. I couldn't replace the broken Tiffany lamp, but I could have the carpet cleaned.

Minutes after David left, I ran my finger down the list of numbers Lois had left for me and called the brothers—Allen and Marvin. The phone rang about ten times before anyone answered.

"Hallow."

"Hi, this is Josephine at the Trippys' house. I have some work for you and your brother."

"Okay."

"Can you guys clean carpets?"

"Yeah."

"Can you be here around noon?"

"Yeah." The unidentified brother hung up the phone.

With that task done, I stepped outside and made sure all the food bowls were full and there was fresh water for everyone. Willy butted my hip, twirled around and leaped over the chaise lounge like a gazelle. Solow tried the same stunt but became stuck, forearms hung down on one side and his back legs searched for purchase on the other side. He looked like he was taking a dry-land swim class. I helped him up and over the chair, laughing out loud the whole time.

Roscoe joined in with a hearty cock-a-doodle-do.

"Quiet, Roscoe...." I listened. Yep, the phone was ringing. I dashed into the kitchen and snagged the house phone.

"Hello."

"Josephine, it's Lois. I hope I wasn't rude to you last night. Either I was dreaming or some crazy things happened in my house."

"You weren't dreaming," I said and bit my lip. I wished I hadn't called her in the first place. After all, the brothers would clean the carpets and sofas and everything would be back to normal, except for the lamp.

"We flew to Rome this morning, and I really want to enjoy this trip. The trouble is, all I can think about is my home in Prunedale. Am I worrying needlessly, Josephine?"

"Yes, everything is now under control here. By the way, did Henry have any visitors other than you and Breana?"

"Well...let's see, Breana of course; Allen and Marvin helped Henry with yard work. Henry's friend, Sam, stopped by once in a while. He was handy at fixing things. I can't think of anyone else."

"How long did Henry know Sam?"

"Henry was a friend of Sam's father. When his father died, Sam kind of looked after Henry, probably the last ten years or so."

"What about Nate?"

"I don't know anyone by that name."

"Squawk, hands up!"

"Quiet, Boris."

"Sorry. I have to go now Josephine." She hung up.

I ignored the bird chatter and called Breana, leaving a message for her to call me. My next call was to Alicia. She sounded better than two days ago, her voice stronger, happier. She invited me over for a cup of tea and Trigger's homemade brownies. I told her I would wait for Allen and Marvin to arrive and then join her for tea.

The brothers arrived with a rented carpet-shampooing machine.

I explained what I wanted them to do, piled Solow into my truck and cruised over to Watsonville, music up, windows down. I parked in front of the Watsonville Market.

"I'll be right back," I said to Solow, leaving the windows down. He couldn't jump out if his life depended on it, but he loved to hang his head out the window and watch the shoppers go by.

It was Robert's day off, so I was back in minutes with a bag of ice cream and a six-pack of root beer.

I drove to Drew Lake Road and curbed the truck in front of Alicia's two-story house in a one-story neighborhood. Trigger greeted us at the front door with hugs and led us to the kitchen.

Little Tansey barked, twirled and leaped, thrilled to have Solow as a guest.

Alicia sat slumped in a chair by the window, staring at Drew Lake.

"Allie, I brought ice cream to go with the brownies."

She turned her head to look at me. "Thanks, Jo, would you mind heating water for tea?" she sighed, adjusting her sling with her left hand.

Where was my optimistic, energetic friend? Who was this sad girl sitting around in her pajamas? Like a bolt of lightening, guilt smacked me square in the heart. It was my fault. If only I had checked the tarps for spiders.

I made the tea and Trigger made himself a root beer float.

Ernie joined us and served up four big brownies and four scoops of vanilla ice cream.

"You know me and ice cream," I said. "It fixes all *my* problems...."

"I hope it fixes Mama's," Trigger said under his breath, between bites.

"Allie, want to go for a ride?"

Solow banged his tail on the floor.

"Not you...Allie."

"I guess...I could take a shower and...."

"Take your time, Allie. We have all afternoon."

"That's right, honey," Ernie said. "Finish your ice cream and then I'll help you to get ready." He gave me a wink. Obviously, he wanted Alicia to go somewhere, do something, anything. "I'll take Trigger fishing on the lake while you're gone."

I told Alicia about a new restaurant in town called Ella's. Since we'd already had dessert, we decided to have a bowl of soup and enjoy a view of the Watsonville Airport runway and green rolling hills in the distance. We discovered there was an art display on the restaurant walls featuring Bonnie Carver, a local watercolorist. As working artists and art appreciators, we always enjoyed seeing other people's artwork.

Carver's colorful, whimsical paintings were fresh and inspiring.

I caught Alicia smiling.

"There was a time when I wanted to be a watercolorist," she said, her eyes glued to an outdoor market scene framed in antiqued silver tones.

"I love the painting, but I would have framed it in…who is that?" I recognized a lady entering the restaurant, but where did I know her from? "Oh, yeah, she works for the jeweler," I said, mostly to myself.

The woman came in alone but was seated with two menus at a table next to our table. She searched her purse for reading glasses and opened a menu.

I turned in my chair and said hello.

"Do I know you?" she asked, looking over her skinny glasses.

"Not really, but I had some work done at the jewelry shop…."

"Yes, now I remember. Don't you hate it when you can't remember names and things? I recently turned fifty and lost my mind. I guess it happens to everyone. I didn't catch your name."

"Josephine, and this is my friend Alicia."

"Julia. I'm new at the shop. My first day on the job was the day you came in. I was so nervous. Between you and me, I'm not sure I want to work there much longer. Sam's the owner and a bit of a nutcase. He's going on a trip, won't tell me where, and he wants me to keep the shop open while he's gone. He has no idea how inept I am," she laughed. "Actually, it was my nephew who put in a good word and got me the job."

"Alonzo told me his aunt worked there. Small world, isn't it?" I glanced at my menu.

"That reminds me, I have to deliver a bunch of papers to Sam before four o'clock. Can you imagine, running errands for the man on Sunday? I don't pay much attention to his personal business, just some real estate papers and his renewed passport. I have it all right here." She patted her bulky purse. "Oh, here comes my friend." Julia stood and hugged her lady friend.

Alicia ordered a garden salad and I ordered the soup of the day.

"Allie, you're working the fork with your left hand pretty well now. Would you like me to cut that hunk of lettuce for you?"

"Thanks, Jo, this has been a humbling experience for me. I've learned to accept help, and I think I understand other people's problems a little better. Now I can relate to people with pain. I've always been healthy...and lucky. I needed this dose of reality, not that I would recommend spider bites to everyone."

"I hope you're not just saying that to make me feel better," I said.

"I'm not, although I do hope you aren't feeling bad about it still."

"Oh, look at that pretty little jet taking off," I said, while silently telling myself to get over the guilt. "Here, I got the check." I put money down on the table.

"You're still feeling guilty, aren't you?" Alicia said as we walked out to the parking lot. "Next time I'm buying."

"Whatever. What did you think of Julia?" I asked as we motored through Watsonville.

"She talks a lot but seems nice enough. If I were Sam, I don't think I'd like my personal information spread around like that."

"Sam, where did I hear that name...?" I slammed on the brakes as an eighteen-wheeler cut over into my lane. "Did you see that?"

"How could I not see it? You look like a mad hornet. Relax and tell me how the painting is going?"

"Alonzo changed his mind about Father Serra. He wants a poker table, a bunch of cowboys and a dance hall girl instead."

"But that's what he already had…a decomposing bar scene."

"People wanted the old painting back. I think he caved under pressure." I made a sharp right and parked in front of Alicia's house. "Need any help, Allie?"

"I'm fine. Thanks for getting me out of my rut." She walked slowly to the front door and slipped inside.

I sat in my idling truck and called David. He picked up on the third ring.

"Are you up to having company?" I asked.

"If you're the company, of course, I am."

"See you in fifteen minutes." We hung up and I drove east to the Aromas hills. Otis Road, shady, hilly, home. I collected mail from my over-flowing mailbox, turned the truck around, drove up David's driveway and cut the engine. I admired the well-kept one story ranch-style house for a moment, remembering good times spent there. The open garage showed off his Jeep, tractor-mower and workbench full of fix-it projects.

A wide swath of apricot trees covered the hillside behind David's house, all the way up to a row of eucalyptus trees stretching westward across the top of the ridge to my house and beyond. His front porch and garden walk were simple but inviting. One large red rhododendron had its back against the house. A row of azaleas lined the brick path.

The front door opened.

David smiled, his hair still wet from a shower. "Josie, glad you could get away from that zoo of yours."

"Actually, I just came from Allie's house. We had lunch. She seems to be doing better, I think."

We entered the house. I spent the first half hour cuddling the kittens and the last two hours cuddling with David.

Sunshine slanted through his kitchen window, reminding me to check my watch. It was dinnertime for the boys at the Trippy house.

"David, I have to get back to Prunedale, but I was wondering...."

"What's on you mind?"

"Your friend at the jewelry shop, does anyone call him Sam?"

"Sure, I do. Is there a problem?"

"No, I was just thinking. How do you know him?"

"Sam, Tom and I used to play golf together once a month in Pacific Grove."

"I remember you told me you used to play...what happened?"

"You." He kissed me. "Don't think and drive," he chuckled.

"Very funny," I said between goodbye kisses. David helped me into the pickup and I reluctantly left Aromas, heading southwest on Highway 101.

Boris welcomed me with "squawk, jabber, jabber, squawk."

"Same to you, old boy." I poked my head out the back door and watched a siesta in action. Willy was stretched out on the chaise lounge, and Solow was fast asleep in the shade under the chair. Roscoe heard me and marched out of the pool shed crowing. In seconds, I had my dog and goat swirling around and through my legs, butting, wagging and telling me how much they loved me and how hungry they were.

When Roscoe and Willy were fed and watered, I took Solow with me into the kitchen. Just as expected, there was a hand-printed bill from the brothers for services rendered. They wanted one hundred dollars. I examined the living room carpet and decided to pay them for a job well done. Finally, I could relax, knowing the Trippy house was in pretty good shape unless you counted Tiffany lamps.

"Boris wants a cracker."

"Okay, Mr. Boris, I'll get you a cracker and fill your food and water and change your newspaper."

"Hands up!"

"Stuff it, Boris."

"Stuff it, Boris, squawk!"

I changed the newspapers at the bottom of the cage. While I was in there, I touched Boris' soft white feathers. He didn't say anything so I continued to pet him.

The phone rang.

I turned to exit the cage.

Boris' knee-jerk reaction was to bite my thumb.

By the time I got to the house phone, little drops of blood had marked my path across the kitchen floor. I picked up the receiver.

"Hello, hello…is any one there…?"

"Hi, Breana, sorry but Bad Boy Boris took a bite out of my thumb. It wasn't his fault. He got a little excited when the phone rang."

"Oh, dear, I'm so sorry…are you bleeding badly?"

"It's going to be okay. What's on your mind, Breana? Everything okay at the hotel?"

"Oh, that part is lovely…I mean, the accommodations are quite sufficient, thank you, Josephine. I was just wonderin' if you'd seen Nate lately."

"No, I haven't seen him since the night you stayed here at the Trippys'. Would you like to come over…?"

"Oh, yes, that would be smashin'. Bless you, I need to talk about things, you know, girl things." She hung up.

I figured it would take Breana at least fifteen minutes to drive to Prunedale, so I put Solow on leash and walked him down the grassy hills to Henry's house. In the dimming light of a recent sunset, I saw a black Harley parked behind Elvira's white Ford pickup. I followed Solow up the porch steps and knocked on the door.

The door opened slowly. Elvira poked her head out.

"Something I can do for you, Josephine?"

"No, I just came down here to see if you needed anything, being new in town and all."

Nate stood behind her. "Josephine, hello... ah, I was just finishing up some chores, cutting firewood and stuff like that."

"Okay, I guess you're doing fine, Elvira. Call me if you need anything." I turned and walked my dog home, wondering what was *really* going on in Henry's house.

Solow and I played with the goat until I heard a car roar up the driveway, sputter and die. Then there was quiet and a door slammed.

Frogs and crickets took up their songs where they left off. I walked around the side of the house on a wide concrete path, passing by a gnome village, an immaculate rose garden and a second community of gnomes. *Who prunes the rose bushes and takes care of the property*, I wondered.

Breana stood at the front door, ready to ring the bell.

"Hi, Breana, let's go this way." I figured the less traffic across the Trippys' damp white carpet the better. She followed me around the house and through the backyard gate. We sat down on a swing-bench near the inky bottomless water hole that smelled like chlorine.

Solow and Willy settled into unconsciousness on the lawn.

Breana finally spoke. "Josephine, I'm truly sorry to be runnin' to you with me every problem...."

"Not a problem. What's going on?"

"It seems I have two suitors—Nate and Alonzo. Alonzo has been, well, let's just say he's on my mind much of the time. Nate, poor boy, hasn't been around, and he doesn't answer my phone calls."

"Do you miss Nate?"

"Well, I'm not sure myself. I guess I worry about him, more of a motherly feelin' you could say."

"How do you feel about Alonzo?" As if I didn't know. She lit up like a twenty-bulb chandelier when I said his name.

"Oh, Josephine, I have only known the man a few days, but my heart beats so hard I can barely catch my breath, it's true. I can't put him out of my mind, not even to get some badly needed sleep...."

"Sounds like love."

"It's not in my plan. I am meant to finish my courses...."

"You can't have Alonzo and finish your classes too?"

Breana squirmed in her seat. "I'm lookin' up at the stars, wonderin' what I'm supposed to do. I don't have a mother to ask and my father never answers my letters. I'm sorry to be burdenin' you, Josephine, truly."

"It's not a burden. Listen to your heart, Breana. Is Alonzo a good person? Will he be true and make you happy? Take your time getting to know him; but if you really love him, don't let him get away." I listened to myself going on and on about love. Why couldn't I settle down with the man I obviously loved?

"You are very wise, Josephine, and I thank ya for takin' the time with me."

If only I could be wise in my own life. David had never popped the question because I always pulled away—spoiled the moment, couldn't face change. But he put up with me anyway.

I walked Breana to her car, never mentioning the fact that Nate was just ten acres away at Henry's house.

Chapter Ten

I woke up Monday morning determined to get all my errands done before I had to go back to work at the Crazy Horse on Tuesday. The house seemed awfully quiet. I opened my eyes and looked across the bedroom at Solow's empty bed.

Smack! Something heavy and breakable obviously hit the tile floor in the kitchen. I yanked the covers off and ran down the hall and through the dining room to the kitchen on bare feet. My jaw dropped as I took in the scene. Solow was running around in circles looking for a place to hide, his tail tucked tightly under his bum.

Boris jumped from counter to table to fridge top to stove top and finally landed on the breakfast bar.

A large clear-glass bowl full of colored sand and a cactus had obviously hit the floor earlier, sending glass and sand everywhere. One white feather wafted slowly through the air, landing on the kitchen table.

"Ouch!" I moaned, feeling something pointy in my right foot. I stepped back from the cactus explosion, leaving a red print on the floor. I decided to clean my cut and put on slippers before attempting to capture Boris.

I called Solow.

"Woof!" He followed me down the hall, tail still tucked.

As I worked at pulling glass and thorns out of my foot, then cleaning and covering my injury, I heard a flap of wings. I stood on one foot and peeked around the corner into the hall. Boris was walk-hopping toward me, chattering unintelligibly. I ignored him, finished bandaging my foot, walked to my bedroom and gingerly shoved my feet into flip flops. My thumb still ached from yesterday's bird bite and now my foot throbbed. Suddenly, as Boris rounded the corner into my room, I was a mad woman, completely out of control.

"Get back, Boris! Shoo, you stupid bird!" I waved my arms and stomped my feet. "Ouch!"

Solow cowered under my bed, probably traumatized for life.

Boris backed off and fast-waddled to the kitchen.

I followed him and saw for the first time that his cage door was open. That was when I had a flashback to the day before when he'd bit my thumb after the phone rang. I remembered closing his door and answering the phone, but I did not remember setting the lock. Now I'd have to replace or pay for a stupid cactus. I grabbed a broom, shooed Boris into his cage, locked his door and began cleaning the kitchen.

"Boris wants a cracker."

"Boris won't get a cracker from me!" I snapped. I immediately felt foolish for taking out my frustration on a poor dumb bird. A bird that spent his whole life locked behind bars.

Once the kitchen was decent, I shuffled through the house in my robe and flip flops to get the morning paper. As I entered the living room and looked around, I realized Boris had been there, making himself at home on the mauve sofas, leaving his poop on the expensive fabric. A fake philodendron plant had big holes chewed in the leaves and the dirt and moss had been tracked across the damp, just cleaned, carpet by a four-legged animal.

The large walnut coffee table looked bare without Lois' fake gladiola arrangement. Three white feathers and a dollop of bird poop remained on the table. I walked to the other side and there was the derangement of glads scattered about the floor. An ornate candy dish had also found its way to the floor, but the candy was gone. Do birds eat candy? I knew for sure that Solow would eat it and probably did. Other than bird poo on the window sills and candy-throw-up near the door, everything was just fine.

I dropped into an over-stuffed chair and let the tears flow. Next thing I knew, Solow was leaning against my thigh whimpering.

"My poor little Solow, this wasn't your fault," I whispered in his ear.

"Squawk!" came from the kitchen. "I know, I know," I moaned, "it was my fault—but *you* took advantage of my forgetfulness."

That was the last straw. I called the brothers and arranged for them to clean house for me. Whichever brother I talked to said, "Okay." I could have spent my day cleaning up after Boris, but I really needed to get my temper under control and run errands so that I'd be fresh for work the following day. At least those were my thoughts at that moment.

I called Mom and told her some of what had happened overnight. I wanted to hear comforting words, not advice like, "Josephine, you should let someone else house sit." She asked if I'd like to go to lunch with her. I said I would because one of my errands was only a few blocks from Mom and Dad's house. Walnut Street dead-ended at the main drag—Pacific Avenue—where Pacific Avenue Jewelers was located. I'd decided to take the ring there, so I wouldn't have to sit around waiting for David to take the ring to his jeweler in Watsonville.

I showered, dressed and tried to eat corn flakes from Lois' pantry, but they stuck in my throat. I finally gave up, fed and watered the boys and left Solow in the backyard to frolic with Willy. I wrote a check for Allen and Marvin for one hundred dollars to cover yesterday's carpet shampooing and laid it on the kitchen table next to the sugar bowl, which reminded me of one of the errands I needed to run. I fingered through the sugar and pulled out the bulky pocket ring, dropped it into my purse and drove to Santa Cruz.

I took the River Street exit into town, made my way down Pacific Avenue and turned right onto Walnut. Two and a half blocks later, I pulled to a stop at the curb in front of my parent's house, the house I'd lived in until I'd married Marty. Sadly, I could barely picture Marty in my mind. Time was washing away old memories, grain by grain, but thankfully, David was always fresh in my mind.

Mom greeted me at the front door, and Dad gave me an extra big hug. Mom must have told him how miserable I was feeling.

"Your mother wants to take you to Chaminade for lunch," Dad said.

"I'm wearing shorts and a tank top. I'm not dressed for anything fancy, Dad. I don't even know if I can eat."

Mom took charge. "Well, dear, we'll just go to the Walnut Bakery then. You always love the food there." Not waiting for my answer, she took my arm and we walked two blocks toward the most heavenly smells on earth. The casual dining began at the sidewalk tables surrounded by flower boxes full of red geraniums. We walked inside and were greeted and seated by a young woman wearing a stretchy tank top, a long black hip-hugging skirt and platform flip flops.

Our eyes traveled all over the menus, even though, as creatures of habit, we already knew what we'd order. I told Mom I had an errand to run on Pacific Avenue a few blocks from the bakery/restaurant. She insisted we walk there together. She said she missed our *girl-time* now that I was spending more time with David. She hinted around to see if he'd asked any important questions, and tried not to look sad when I said there hadn't been any such questions.

We each ordered our favorite chicken walnut salad and a *fresh from the oven* apple turnover for dessert. I felt comforted by my mother's familiar stories and trivia and by the good food. Mom paid the bill and we began our walk down the street.

"This is going to be fun, honey! I haven't been to the Pacific Avenue Jewelers in years."

"Me either. The last time I was there was to have my wedding ring sized." Twenty-seven years later, Marty was just a sweet memory. "Mom, wait a minute! I want to make sure the ring is…."

As I fished around in the bottom of my purse, I felt the ring and pulled it up to daylight.

A tinny-sounding bell became louder and more obnoxious.

"Jo, look out!" Mom yelled, as a curly-headed teen bicycled by us, ringing his little bike bell as he cut in and out of crowds of strolling pedestrians.

In slow motion, I saw red stripes on silver metal.

"Honey, are you okay?" Mom smoothed my hair back and looked into my startled face. "Did the bike hit you, dear?"

"Just my toe; a bad day to be wearing flip flops."

"You look so pale."

"Mom…it's just that…." I stared into my empty hand, mouth gaping, eyes tearing. I dropped down on my haunches and searched the sidewalk, dodging foot traffic all around us. "Mom, I dropped the ring!"

"What ring, honey?"

"The big blue ring I told you about, very old, must find...ouch! That was my finger. Watch where you're walking!"

A startled young woman turned around ready to defend herself.

"Sorry, I lost something," I explained to the stranger. Could the ring have rolled to the gutter? I crawled another three feet to the edge of the sidewalk and looked down into a storm drain. A grate consisting of a dozen metal rods spaced an inch apart was securely fastened over the sewer opening. I imagined the ring rolling through one of the one-inch spaces. The sewers collected rainwater and sent it to the ocean. Luckily, we hadn't had rain in several months.

I imagined a lucky scuba diver finding the ancient ring at the bottom of the Pacific Ocean, and almost laughed at the irony—the ring had originally come from a ship on the Atlantic Ocean. Now it was probably on its way back to sea on the other side of the world.

I stood up. My head spun. My lunch lurched.

"Honey, are you okay?" Mom asked. She took my arm and led me to the shady side of a large stone building, away from foot traffic.

"I'm not okay, Mom. I have to find that ring! It doesn't belong to me."

"Let's finish your errand and go back to the house and rest."

"That *was* my errand. I was taking the ring to another jeweler for a second opinion."

"All right, let's go home," she said gently, as we turned down Walnut Avenue. Back at the house, Mom explained to Dad why I was curled in a ball on the sofa, moaning about the complete ruination of my life on planet earth.

"Don't worry, honey, I'm going to call my friend at the water department. I've known him for years." He disappeared into the den for several minutes and returned with a naughty smile on his face.

"What happened, Bob?" Mom asked.

"Talked to my friend, reminded him of the times I subbed on his bowling team. He agreed to send a guy out to open up the drain. He should be here at the house in an hour."

"Thanks, Dad. I'm feeling better already. I think I'll go for a little drive before the guy shows up." They wanted me to stay and rest but I convinced them I needed to go. I drove down Pacific Avenue, searching for the curly-haired guy on a bike with a red stripe of paint over a silver fender. I tried some side streets and Pacific Avenue again. He could be anywhere.

I decided to make a quick drive to the boardwalk. On the way, I saw the curly-headed kid talking to a girl carrying a surfboard. He pushed his bike as they walked along the sidewalk. I pulled to a stop a couple of car lengths ahead and let them walk to me. I climbed out of the truck, stepped onto the sidewalk and said a friendly hello. They paused for a moment and kept walking.

"Hey, I need to talk to you," I said, rushing up to the boy.

He stopped. "Like, do I know you?" he asked.

Surfer Girl continued walking.

"You ran into me on the sidewalk." I pointed back to Pacific Avenue.

"I didn't hit anyone…"

"You didn't hit me, but you ran over my toe and knocked a ring out of my hand. Do you remember that?"

"Actually, I saw a big blue ring roll into the drain."

"Thanks, that's all I needed to know." I felt a bit sorry for the young man, looking for his *surfer girl* who was, by that time, two blocks away.

I quickly motored back to my parent's house and parked behind an official white pickup from the water department. All my hopes rested on the meter man.

Dad introduced me to a rather hefty balding man wearing a tight blue meter man uniform and black rubber boots. He asked if I'd show him the storm drain. I said I'd be glad to. He escorted me to his little pickup truck, held the door open and helped me into my seat with all the nervous pomp of a young man going to his first prom. Maybe he didn't notice my limping gate, black toe, skinned knees and red puffy eyes.

Mr. Meter Man followed my directions to the storm drain and parked five feet away. He cracked my window open a few inches, and fetched a metal bar and a stack of orange cones from the truck bed. I watched from the cab as he pulled on rubber gloves and arranged four cones around the perimeter of the sewer. Using the bar, he leveraged the grate up a few inches and moved it to one side.

I tried to be positive. Over and over, I visualized the man holding up a blue and gold ring. But eventually, my mind slipped into reverse. I imagined that Elvira had me strapped to a telephone pole. She smeared peanut butter all over me and let Willy lick it off. Because I have a low tolerance for tickles, the goat was killing me. I figured Elvira would bury me in the shade of an old oak tree before anyone knew I was missing.

My mind snapped back to the present as the sun threatened to burn a hole in the windshield. I tried again to focus on a good outcome. I pulled the headliner down and watched dust particles dance in the hot air. I sneezed, opened my eyes and there he was at my window.

"Okay, drains open, what are we looking for?"

"A heavy gold ring with a big blue stone."

I think he rolled his eyes, probably thinking back to his boyhood and a Penny Arcade plastic souvenir ring he gave his mother, but I'm not sure. He turned back to the open hole and stepped down a couple of feet into it. I watched as he immediately raised one foot, reached down and picked up something.

I held my breath.

He wiped the thing on his shirt and inspected it.

I was still holding my breath, but once I saw sunlight on blue and gold, I sucked in some air and thanked God for huge favors. I thanked the meter man, took the ring and told him I didn't need a ride back to the house—that I needed some fresh air and would walk. One minute he was smiling like Sir Lancelot, the next minute like he'd fallen off his horse.

I waved and smiled as the little white pickup pulled into traffic.

After a couple of swipes with my shirttail, the ring sparkled.

Since I was now only a few yards from the Pacific Avenue Jewelers' ornately-etched glass doors, I held the ring in my fist and hustled into the high fashion, grandiose supermarket of jewelry for the rich and famous. A woman dressed in a simple black dress and diamond necklace approached me and asked if I needed a battery for my watch.

"No, I don't need a battery…."

Her eyes went from my wristwatch and bandaged thumb, to my skinned knees and black toe. Reflected in the glass showcase were my fly-away hair, red-rimmed eyes and a black smudge on my face I hadn't noticed before.

I opened my fist and showed her the ring. "I need an expert to look at this."

Her nose wrinkled and her lips pruned when she saw the dirty old ring. "Oh, my, I'll see if Mr. Louden has a moment." She wiggled across the room on high heels and disappeared into another room. Moments later, she was back with an irritated man wearing a jeweler's loupe strapped to his forehead, who looked ready to throw another homeless beggar out the door.

"May I see the ring?" he said in a tired voice.

I handed it to him.

Instantly, he seemed surprised by the weight of it.

"Looks like glass," he said. He opened the ring's top and his jaw dropped. Suddenly, his eyes were lusting over the ring. "Where did you find this?" he asked in a tone that insinuated the ring was not mine. Actually, it wasn't but I didn't like the tone.

"I've had the ring for a while and I'm wondering if it has a history. I know that it's just blue glass, but what about the rest of it?"

"To tell you the truth, I know the history of this very ring. Obviously, someone has replaced the sapphire with glass. But the ring is still worth...ah...quite a bit, but nothing compared to the missing stone. This is a Bezel-style hinged ring from the Renaissance period. Specifically, it was part of Captain Stone's bootie, seized from a French ship in the Gulf of Mexico around 1750." He pulled the loupe down over one eye and re-examined the ring. Beads of perspiration broke out across his forehead.

Louden pushed the loupe higher on his forehead and started to turn away.

"That's great, thanks a lot," I said, reaching for the ring in his hand.

He curled his fingers and pulled away.

"I have to go now...where are you going with my ring?"

Louden and the woman walked briskly toward the room he'd come from minutes ago.

I caught up to them and asked for the ring.

She sneered over her shoulder.

He told me he had to make a phone call before he could give it back.

With visions of police stations and Elvira shaking her fist at me, my only other thought was to stop this man and get the ring back. I swung my purse hard into his hand. The ring dropped on the super shiny hardwood floor, bounced and rolled about twenty feet. The woman shrieked and Louden gasped in disbelief, giving me a chance to be first to get to the ring. I scooped it up on-the-fly, dashed out the front door and down the sidewalk, legs pumping like a marathon runner.

A cluster of street people cheered me on, "Run, lady, run!" as my flip flops flap, flap, flapped on concrete. I ran four blocks, zigzagging around shoppers and gawkers, made a right, crossing the street onto Chestnut and then over to Walnut. I raced around my folk's house to the backyard, because ringing the doorbell might take too long. Someone might see me. In my imagination, there was already an APB out on me and a fleet of patrol cars was cruising the streets of Santa Cruz.

I pounded on the sliding glass door and Dad let me in.

"Honey, what…?" he stammered as I shot through the door and dropped into a chair, breathless.

I opened my fist and showed Dad the ring. "They were going to call the police…so I grabbed the ring…and ran all the way. Turns out, this ring is worth a lot…even without the sapphire. Maybe someone murdered Henry for this…." I held it up for Dad to see.

"What do you mean, you grabbed the ring?"

"Actually, I whacked the jeweler, Mr. Fancy Pants. Swatted his hand with my purse—the one you think looks like real alligator." I held the purse up as *Exhibit*

A. "You should have seen the woman's face! Louden looked pretty upset too. The ring rolled across the room and I made a really fast dash for it. Six blocks later, here I am!"

Mom walked into the room. "Did I hear you say something about Mr. Louden?"

"I was just telling Dad about...taking the blue ring to the jeweler. I'm a little out of breath...because I decided to get some exercise...and jog back to the house."

Mom nodded knowingly. "Exercise is good. How about a cup of tea and you can tell me what Mr. Louden said about the ring?"

That much I would tell her, the rest was between Dad and me.

Chapter Eleven

Hitchcock's classic, *North by Northwest* kept me awake way too long Monday night. Cary Grant reminded me of David who was just as attractive in my mind, just not quite as polished. I spent the evening in the now brand spanking clean Trippy house with Solow, popcorn, ice cream and Cary Grant.

Mom had asked me to stay for dinner, but I needed to get back to my boys. I'd promised myself that I'd spend more time with Boris, and, so far, that hadn't happened. Maybe he'd escaped captivity and gone berserk in Lois' living room because I had neglected him. Thankfully, Solow, Willy and Roscoe had each other.

The brothers had done a fine job cleaning the living room and had left a bill for one hundred dollars on the kitchen table. I saw it as I dropped the blue ring into the sugar bowl.

The next day, I was lying in bed. It was Tuesday morning and I was trying to remember if I'd pushed the ring down under the sugar, when the doorbell rang.

Solow woofed.

I glanced at the clock. Good grief, it was already nine o'clock! The bell rang again. I leaped out of bed, pulled on my robe and hurried to the front door. I looked through the peek hole and discovered Elvira, reading the front page of my newspaper. As soon as I opened the door, she rolled it up and handed it to me.

"Thanks; now I don't have to go hunting for it," I said.

"Your state sure has a durn funny attitude about things. Good thing I live in Texas," she laughed, or was that a cackle? "Actually, I'm here to borrow a cup ah sugar—got any?"

My cheeks went from waking-up-pale to hot-and-pink.

"Ah, sure, come in." I led her into the kitchen and began opening cupboards, hoping to find a sack or canister full of sugar. I opened the pantry door and turned on the light.

"Hey girl! What's this? Sure looks like a sugar bowl ta me...."

"Oh, of course...why didn't I think of that?" I said as I darted across the room and stretched my arm over the table to reach one of the handles on the little two-handle sugar bowl. For a moment, we each had a handle. Seconds seemed like hours. Finally, she let go. Thankfully, all I saw was sugar when I lifted the lid a tiny bit.

"Do you want me to take the bowl?" Elvira asked.

I'd rather be eaten alive by termites, I thought. Keeping a smile pasted on my face, I said, "Just a minute; I'll find a container to put some sugar in...since this is the only sugar we have."

"Oh, my; I wouldn't take all your sugar! I just need a smidgeon for mah coffee."

I held the sugar bowl against my belly while searching cupboards and drawers for a container. I opened the fridge and searched every shelf, remembering the piles of sugar, flour and salt on the kitchen floor at Henry's house the day it was ransacked. In desperation, I finally pulled out a small container of yogurt, dumped the contents into the sink, wiped the plastic container clean and dry and then scooped some sugar into it with a spoon, being careful to keep the ring inside the sugar bowl.

Elvira cocked her head to one side.

"I still don't know where things are around here," I explained. "This will have to do."

She smiled.

Was she trying to be neighborly? I didn't have time for stuff like that. I had to get ready for work.

She took the yogurt container and drove away in her truck.

It was ten o'clock when I curbed my truck and cut the engine in front of the Crazy Horse Saloon.

Kyle roared to a stop a minute later and helped me carry equipment into the building.

Blinking and straining to see in the dim light, I saw three people coming down the narrow wooden stairs single-file.

Breana pounded down the stairs into the main dining room with Alonzo close behind.

"Josephine, Alonzo has been showing me around town. I even saw the underground tunnel. It's blocked now, but it used to go all the way over to the mission. And we walked around the mission; a lovely tour it was!" she gushed.

I looked to see who the third person was, but there was only Breana and Alonzo.

"That's wonderful, Breana! I hope to look around town when I have some time." I set my ladder in place and squeezed a couple of greens, some burnt sienna, yellow, cobalt blue, red, white and black onto my palette.

I'd only painted a few minutes when two silhouettes, back-lit by the morning sun, came through the door, one tall and slim, the other heavy-set, dark skinned and going gray. The skinny blond asked Alonzo if I worked in his restaurant.

"Josephine, someone to see you," Alonzo said, off-handedly.

"Right here, officers," I said with careful politeness as I back-stepped down the ladder.

"Ms. Stuart, step outside, please," Officer Lund said.

I walked with them out into the sunshine, eyes tearing from the intense light.

"Into the back seat," she said, as Officer Sayer held the door open for me.

I hesitated.

"Please, Ms. Stuart."

I climbed in.

The officers sat in the front seats, closed the doors and we talked.

"What is this all about?" I said indignantly.

"A camera at the Pacific Avenue Jewelers shows you accosting the owner, Mr. Louden," Sayer said. "He claims you are in possession of a stolen ring."

"How did you know it was me? I didn't tell Mr. Louden anything about myself."

"We recognized you when the film was played on Channel 8 last night," Sayer said, holding back a grin.

"Louden had *my* ring and wouldn't give it back to me. I wasn't about to let him keep it. What right did he have to keep *my* ring?"

"Do you have the ring now?" Lund asked in her usual frosty tone.

"No, I don't have it with me. What's the big deal about this ring anyway?"

"We're just following up on the complaint," Sayer said in a much warmer tone. "You say Mr. Louden refused to give the ring back to you?"

"That's right."

Sayer jotted something into his notebook, stepped out of the car and helped me out of the back seat. As I stood on the sidewalk wondering what would happen next, Officer Sayer said, "Nice maneuver with the purse," under his breath.

"Thanks. Any news on who murdered Henry?"

"We're working on it." He dropped into the passenger seat, slammed the door and Lund hit the gas. *She'd be a great cop if she had an attitude adjustment,* I thought to myself, and smiled as they disappeared down the street. Since I was already outside the building, I took a few minutes to walk up the sidewalk to the Jewelry Company. There was that *closed* sign again. Maybe Rotsider had gone on a trip like Julia had talked about. But where was *she*?

I walked back to the restaurant and climbed my ladder.

"Can you give the horse a white diamond on his forehead?" Alonzo asked. "I had a horse like that when I was a kid."

"No problem. The horse will be all one color at first, and then I'll add shadows, highlights, the mane, tail and the diamond. It's a process."

Alonzo smiled and walked Breana out to her car. It was at least half an hour before he came back.

Following my own pencil lines, I quickly painted in the muscular, bucking chestnut horse. Adding lights, darks, tail, and mane took the rest of the day to complete.

Kyle had added more cattle and some realistic-looking dust to his painting. One more day and he'd be finished—in more ways than one. His work at the Crazy Horse would be complete, but, of course, I'd use him again on future projects.

When it was almost five o'clock, Kyle and I hauled our equipment to the truck. He pulled his helmet on and rode north toward Santa Cruz. As I began the first block of my drive to Prunedale, I noticed an *open* sign at the

Jewelry Company and Julia standing near the door—coming or going—I could only guess.

I quickly parked and walked a few steps to the door.

"Hi, Julia! Are you closing up?"

"No, I was just about to go out for a quick cup of coffee." She thumbed the bakery next door. "Would you like to join me? I'm supposed to keep the shop open until seven, but I'm falling asleep on my feet."

"Sure, let's go!" We entered the bakery minutes before they closed. The cashier gave us day-old, bottom of the pot coffee in paper cups and day-old donuts, which we carried back to the jewelry shop. We sat on stools behind the showcase and talked. Julia told me about her life—fifty years of it. I finally was able to say a few words and asked her about Rotsider's vacation. She said that Sam had been scheduled to fly to Paris that morning. Since Julia was a congenital motor-mouth, I believed her when she said that was all she knew about Rotsider.

"Must be nice," I said, wishing I were on a plane to Paris. "Does he have a family, wife, anybody?"

"I don't think so, but I don't know for sure. He's a very private person—not like me," she laughed, and daintily dunked her last piece of donut.

"Did you happen to see Mr. Rotsider working on my ring?"

"Huh? Oh, the big blue ring? What do you mean, work on it? He just dropped it in a drawer. Maybe he worked on it when I wasn't around. One of my jobs is to clean the jewelry that comes in, so, of course, *I* worked on your ring, cleaning it, that is."

"Do you know very much about the ring, like its history, stuff like that?" I asked.

"I'm no history buff, Josephine, but I know an antique when I see one. Your ring is very beautiful. Did you inherit it?"

"Actually, I'm just keeping it for someone. That reminds me, I need to get back to my boys."

"How many boys do you have?"

"I have a dog, a cockatoo, a rooster and a goat." I walked to the door. "See you later, Julia. Thanks for coffee and donuts!" I hurried to my truck and motored over to Prunedale, my mind focused on the ring as usual. *What was it about that old ring? Did it have me in its power?* I asked myself as I pulled to a stop at the Trippys' house. I crept through the living room and dining room, wondering what new messes or disasters might be waiting for me. I entered the kitchen, happy to see everything in its place.

"Hands up...squawk!"

"Hey, old buddy, Boris!" I stuck my fingers in the sugar bowl just to make sure the ring was there. "What is it about this ring, Boris?"

"Give me the ring!" he squawked.

"What did you say? You *do* know about this ring, don't you? Maybe I should listen to you more often."

"Squawk!"

I'd already decided that Henry had died at the hands of someone trying to steal his ring. What if the ring had originally had a real sapphire instead of glass? It might be worth millions. *That* would be a motive for murder. Did Henry quickly drop the ring in a sack of oats to hide it from someone he didn't trust and that was how Willy ended up eating it? If there really was a sapphire in it originally, where did it go and who'd replaced the gemstone with glass? It would take a jeweler to do that. "A jeweler! Oh my God!"

I went through the motions of feeding, watering and loving the boys, but my mind was fixated on the notion that somewhere out there, there was a real sapphire and someone mean enough to kill for it. Maybe it was all *my* fault. Maybe Rotsider had kept the ring for three days so he'd have time to locate or make a glass replacement. An ocean of guilt suddenly washed over me when I fully realized *I* was person who'd enabled the jeweler to steal the precious stone! Was *he* the murderer?

On the other hand, what if Henry took the ring to the jewelry shop for cleaning or repair? Maybe Rotsider knew all about the valuable ring, and went to Henry's home and murdered him. Ironically, he didn't get the ring when he killed him, but in the end *I* made sure he got the sapphire. I just didn't know.

I called Breana and asked if she'd join me for an evening of ice cream, popcorn and a movie. She said she had homework. I said, "Fine, no worries!" I hung up the phone. Fifteen minutes later, Breana rang the doorbell. I let her in.

"Somethin's up with you; what is it, Josephine? I'm thinkin,' should I be here? But I see dark clouds in your eyes, I do. Always could read a face…."

"Thanks for coming, Bree. I'm feeling really bad, and I want to tell you all about it. I need to get some things off my chest. I'll make us some tea and sandwiches first."

Breana divided her time between the needy boys— Solow and Boris—while I put together a light dinner.

"Lois will be happy, she will, the way you keep her house neat as a pin."

"Thanks, Bree, but I hired the brothers to clean— twice, actually. The house was broken into and then I accidentally left Boris' cage door unlocked and the house was a disaster when I woke up Monday morning. It's costing me a fortune to keep all this white carpet clean," I said as I sliced the crust off our sandwiches.

"This is lookin' like the Queen's tea with all the trouble you're goin' to."

"Hope you like bologna and cucumber, not exactly the Queen's fare."

"Just spill whatever it is that's makin' ya feel so sad, girl. I'm here to listen," she said, spreading a napkin across her lap. We were working on dessert by the time I finished explaining my theory about Henry's murder and stolen sapphire.

Boris had been unusually quiet and Solow napped under the table.

We helped ourselves to multiple squirts of chocolate syrup and whipped cream on our ice cream. Serious subjects required serious sweets.

"Josephine, I don't feel so good."

"Me too. I can't finish this sweet stuff," I groaned and pushed the bowl away.

"Squawk...sweet stuff...squawk!"

"Wow, he really pays attention to what we say," Breana said.

"I think he witnessed the murder—after all, his cage was right there in Henry's living room! Boris says things like *back up now* and *hands up*. Or maybe he just picks up phrases from TV movies." I shrugged.

"He's really a sweet old bird; wish he were mine," she smiled.

"I do too. I mean, you're right—sweet old bird. Breana, I know you don't know Nate real well, but isn't Nate short for Nathan?"

"Yes, it is. Haven't seen 'im in a while. I think he's given up on me, truly he has."

"My mother has been looking into Henry's family history. His sister's granddaughter—that would be Elvira—had a baby boy named Nathan. We don't know if he lived or not. Mom thinks he would be 22 years old now. Elvira assured me that she's the only living heir to Henry's estate. But having a guy named Nate hanging around Henry's property is quite a coincidence."

"It certainly is a coincidence, and Nate just happens to be 22 years old," Breana said, thoughtfully.

My skin prickled all the way down to my feet. "Are you sure he's out of the picture, Bree? Wouldn't you like to have one more date with him?"

"He's not a bad chap; I rather liked him...." Her eyelids dropped, her head tilted to one side. "What are ya dreamin' up, Josephine?"

"Just call him and go out one more time. You might want to ask him where he was born, does he have any family around here, you know, stuff like that."

"Did *he* kill Henry?" Her eyes went squinty, mouth in a pout.

"No, no, nothing like that. I just want to know if he's Elvira's son."

I watched Solow tread water in his dreams, under the table.

"Boris wants a cracker."

"Okay, coming right up." I made chamomile tea, added some cold water to it and placed the cup in the bottom of the cage.

"He'll be sleepin' on his feet in no time," Breana laughed. "A bit tired meself."

"Bree, it was so nice of you to come over. I really needed to share my thoughts with you. I feel better now."

"T'was a lovely meal, but I should be on me way if ya don't mind."

"Alonzo is a nice guy," I smiled, as her cheeks pinked.

"He surely is. I'm a bit sweet on him," she grinned. "But I'll see if I can make one last date with Nate. Curious too, I am."

I walked Breana to her car. "Bree, did you ever notice Henry wearing a big gold ring with a blue stone?"

Even in twilight I saw her cheeks redden.

"I noticed it all right, big ol' thing that it was. Wore it on his middle finger and even then it always fell to one side. I suppose Henrietta's fingers were smaller than the real Henry's."

"Did you know that about twenty years ago Henry went to Texas and died in his sister's house?"

She shook her head of curls.

"That was when Henrietta saw her big chance to come to California."

"So *that's* how it happened. Of course, I never met the real Henry. I was just a babe when he was alive. Henrietta will always be Henry to me. Very kind person he, ah, *she* was." She climbed into her car and said, "Goodnight."

Solow and I watched the taillights disappear. The evening air wafted the sour scent of a swindle, a barbeque somewhere in the neighborhood and jasmine from the fence. Solow followed me to the backyard for a romp with Willy. I settled into a chaise lounge, gazed up at smears of blood red commingling with mandarin orange across the western end of a deep purple sky and marveled at how easily Henrietta had taken over everything *Henry*.

I heard a car motor and then a door slam.

Solow stopped his play and barked.

We rounded the house and met up with Breana at the front door.

"Oh, Josephine, didn't see you there! I came back because I saw Nate. Just as I came to a stop at the bottom of the drive, he zoomed out of Henry's road onto Langley. I recognized the motorcycle and the helmet...it was him all right. Seems he spends a lot of time at Henry's place, he does," she said breathlessly. "Do you think he did harm to poor old Henry—Henrietta?"

"I don't know him that well. What do you think?"

"It's a funny thing, but he didn't tell me much about himself, but I told him everything about myself," she sighed.

I walked Breana to her car. "Thanks, Bree, I guess we don't need to ask Nate anything after all. We know that he and his mother have been lying to us. You told me once that Nate was the one who found Henry's body. I wonder if the investigators on the case know about that."

"The truth is, Nate said he'd arrived at Henry's just minutes before I drove up. I saw poor Henry on the floor...dead." She hung her head.

I gave her a hug. "Don't worry; if Nate's innocent the sheriff will figure it out." I felt relief that my friend would not be risking her safety snooping around in Nate's private life.

Chapter Twelve

It was the middle of the week, hump-day for most people, but for me it would be four more days of painting at the Crazy Horse. The bucking horse picture was finished; time to move on to the dance hall girl and poker game. I wished Alicia could help me with it, but I knew she wasn't able. She still handled most chores awkwardly using her left hand.

The days of September were getting warmer. Tuesday night, after Breana went home, I'd worried that my mural paint might boil and be ruined under the metal cover on my truck. I decided to use the empty space in the Trippy garage that had been offered to me before the couple left on their trip. Lois had left the automatic door opener on the kitchen counter in case I changed my mind. I fastened it to the visor in my truck, opened the door and parked alongside Tom's silver Tesla.

I closed the garage door and walked toward the kitchen door, but the Tesla stopped me. Its lines were so pretty. I put my face to the glass and ogled the leather seats, the futuristic dash and what was that on the seat? I opened the car door. A rank stench hit my nostrils, like being down wind of three tons of chicken manure.

"Oh, my…this is nasty!" I pinched the top of a greasy paper bag from Barry's Barbecue, dropped it in a garbage can by the back door and rolled the can outside.

Solow sniffed the can and followed me into the garage.

"Believe me, you don't want that rotted food." But his tail wagged as his eyes pleaded. I walked back to the Tesla to close the door and noticed crumpled paper on the floor in front of the passenger seat. I straightened the pink receipt and turned the paper so I could read it. The Jewelry Company, San Juan Bautista, California. "Looks like the Trippys traded with Mr. Rotsider." I remembered his steel-blue eyes, streaked gray hair and long boney fingers.

Solow yawned.

I called him into the house, spread the receipt on the kitchen counter and read the scribbley handwriting as best I could. It seemed Tom or Lois had purchased a watch battery on July 13. The amount of money paid was five hundred dollars. *No big deal there*, I thought.

"Boris wants a cracker."

"Boris, ever see a watch with a five-hundred-dollar battery?"

He cocked his head to one side.

I thought about my situation compared to the Trippys' good fortune in life's lottery. My watch was a Timex. When the battery wore out, I would simply buy a new watch for twenty bucks. Tom had studied hard and worked his way up the IBM ladder until his retirement. I too had worked hard, but I didn't expect to be rich any time soon.

The house phone rang.

"Hello."

"Squawk!"

"Be quiet, Boris!"

"Josephine, is everything all right? Is Boris behaving?"

"Hi, Lois; he's fine, just noisy sometimes. Where are you calling from?"

"We took the train to Munich this morning. I just wanted to know if everything is okay at the house."

"Your house is fine. Did I tell you that the police think Henry was murdered?"

"Oh, dear…murder you say?"

"Do you know anything about Nate?"

"Are you talking about the Nate who split wood for Henry?"

"Yes, the one who was dating Breana," I said.

"Maybe they did the murder together."

"Lois, you don't mean that. Breana's a very sweet girl."

"I'm just speculating, Josephine. Have the brothers taken good care of the property—mowing and trimming?"

"I haven't seen them working, but the lawn looks great. Solow and Willy love to romp on it…."

"Willy?"

"Ah, I told you about him. He's a little goat, very well behaved actually…he belonged to Henry."

"Oh. Are you keeping him?"

"No, you are…I mean, he comes with the bird." I wiped my sweaty forehead with the back of my hand.

"I have to go," Lois snapped, and hung up the phone.

After a hurried round of chores, I backed the truck out of the garage, rounded the giant oak and headed down the driveway. At the bottom of the drive, I noticed a faded red Chevy pickup parked at the side of Langley Gulch Road. Two men wearing hats and sunglasses crouched in their seats. One had a familiar-looking mustache.

A mile later, I noticed the truck was behind me. It continued following me all the way to San Juan Bautista, but kept going when I pulled to the curb at the Crazy Horse. A lawnmower rolled backward into the tailgate as the Chevy picked up speed and left town.

The brothers were shadowing me. I was still laughing when Kyle leaned down to my open window.

"Do you ever just laugh for no reason?" I asked.

"Ah, not really…this *is* payday, right?"

"Sure is. All you have to do is finish the painting." I thought about the seven dollars plus change in my purse, empty checkbook and low bank balance. I would ask Alonzo for some cash. "Kyle, go ahead and unload the truck."

Alonzo stood on the sidewalk waiting for me.

"Josephine, what do you know about this Nate character?"

"Why? Was he here? Where's Bree?" My voice trembled.

"I thought so!" Alonzo curled his hands into fists. "There's something wrong with this guy, right?"

"Maybe not—I don't really know him that well. Where did they go?" I spotted Breana's car parked at the curb halfway between the Jewelers and the Crazy Horse.

Alonzo explained to me that Nate had approached Breana, asking if he could drive her to her nursing class. At first, she'd said *no* but later changed her mind and left with him in a white Ford 350. I waited another minute for Kyle to finish hauling our equipment into the restaurant and then told Alonzo that I'd be back shortly. Actually, I had no idea when I'd be back.

Without an invitation, Alonzo climbed into the passenger seat and slammed the door with twice the force needed. We were of one mind—bring Breana back safely. My little truck tore through the countryside like a rabid dog with no idea where it was going. Alonzo suggested we try the nursing school in Salinas. He knew how to get there and put me on the right set of roads.

Once we arrived at the school, Alonzo ran into the building while I drove through the three sections of parking lot looking for a white Ford pickup. I learned one thing—not many nurses drive pickup trucks.

After a while, I saw Alonzo coming from the building. He stepped off the sidewalk and climbed into the passenger seat. He said he'd tried to enter a classroom, but was told to leave the campus. Our next stop was my idea—Henry's place. The cab was mummy quiet giving me time to think. Did Breana go with Nate because I'd asked her to question him? What was a little more guilt when I was already up to my hubcaps in it?

"Hey, Josephine, buck up," Alonzo said. "If she didn't go to class, we'll find her!"

"You're right, we'll find her. Thanks for coming with me."

"Langley Gulch Road; I've been here before," he said with his jaw set, eyes straight ahead.

A moment later, we were roaring up Henry's driveway, gravel smacking the wheel wells, dust engulfing the landscape behind us. I pulled the truck onto a grassy patch and killed the engine a hundred feet short of the house. We walked past Elvira's white pickup and up three creaky wooden stairs to the mossy front porch. A curtain in the front window moved. The front door opened.

I smelled fresh perked coffee and garlic fries.

"Elvira, uh, we were just wondering why Breana didn't go to her class," I sputtered.

She turned and spoke to Nate who was standing behind her, "Nate, do you know anything about Breana goin' to class?"

"I dropped her off. What's the big deal?" Nate walked up behind his mother, looking cocky. "I wanted her to spend some time with me, but she insisted on going to her stupid little class. Now I have to pick her up at four o'clock."

Elvira stepped back. "Come on in, folks. I plumb forgot my manners."

Alonzo gave me a two-finger push from behind as we entered the living room. I could feel his worry and anger through the fingers in my back.

Elvira, Nate, I'd like you to meet my friend, Alonzo Alvarez...."

"I know who he is," Nate growled. "Bree has no taste, goin' for a wetba...."

"Bam!" Alonzo's fist snapped Nate's chin up and back, throwing him backward over an ottoman, long legs flailing as he fell into a rickety rocking chair. He lay on top of broken sticks and spindles to his mother's horror. She bent down and pulled her son to his feet.

"Boys, take it outside!" She thumbed towards the front door and stepped aside, letting them stomp out the door and down the steps. "Now, Josephine, what's this all about?"

I ignored the cussing and fighting outside, and concentrated on the six-foot tall woman in front of me. Her face was redder than I remembered, and her eyes were wild like a coyote locked in a hatchery. I felt like I was ten years old again, trying to explain to Miss Brundy that the hamster ate my homework—a paper maché rendition of the Santa Cruz Mission.

"So, Elvira, is Nate your son?"

"Been muh son for twenty-two years. Is that a problem?" Her eyes squinted down to little slits.

"No, no problem, it's just that you told me you were Henry's, ah, Henrietta's only heir...." I backed up to the front window, turned my head and took a quick peek to see if the boys were still alive.

They were gone.

She put her hands to her hips. "I *am* my grandmother's only heir and Nate is *my* only heir."

"I also know that you identified Henrietta's body and Nate was the one who found her dead...."

"Are you tryin' to prove somethin,' Josephine?" She moved closer.

I smelled garlic fries on her breath as she spoke:

"I thought we was friends. I borrowed sugar from you. I even stood up for you when the brothers accused you of stealin' the family ring."

"Huh? How do you know the brothers and how do you know *they* didn't take the ring?"

"Allen and Marvin used to work for my grandmother, and out of respect, they drop by now and then. Yesterday, they brought the mail. Real gentlemen, I'd say." She stuck her big hand out. "Friends?"

We shook hands. It felt more like Miss Brundy and the hamster all over again. I wondered if anyone offered a class on "how to conquer guilt."

"We best find those boys before they do permanent damage to each other." She laughed as she opened the front door and clapped her hands. "Sooie! Little pigs, git your butts over here!" she hollered with enough force to uproot a redwood. We stood on the porch waiting for the guys to appear.

First Nate slunk around the corner of the house, head down, lip bloody, with hands in pockets.

Next came Alonzo, six inches shorter than Nate but puffed up like a rooster with a black eye.

"Okay, boys, shake hands...you heard me," Elvira shouted from the porch.

Alonzo caught up to Nate and put his hand out.

Nate shook the offered hand. They turned their backs to us and walked together to the barn where Willy had once lived.

Elvira led me back inside for a cup of coffee.

"Sugar? Cream?" Elvira asked.

"Sugar, please."

She plucked two little cubes of sugar from an ugly brown mug and dropped them into my coffee. I wondered what had happened to the yogurt container full of sugar.

We sat at the table discussing the weather and our family histories. My history was short and dry, but Elvira talked about her great, great, great, great grandfather—the colorful Captain Stone who'd fought as a privateer to protect the gulf coast from pirates, but eventually became a pirate himself. She figured Henry had unofficially inherited the family treasure but probably spent it. The only piece of it she'd ever seen was a sapphire ring. Elvira admitted that six years ago, when she came out west for a visit, the ring had fascinated her as it glinted and glowed on her grandmother's middle finger.

Driving Alonzo back to his saloon, I wondered if Henrietta had promised to leave the ring to Elvira. Lois must have seen the ring too. I made a mental note to ask her about it.

While I had Alonzo in my truck, I asked him if he'd pay me enough money to pay Kyle for his work since it was his last day of painting. Alonzo said he'd write a check directly to Kyle.

It was noon when we finally walked into the Crazy Horse.

"Hey, Josephine! What do you think? Do I add, like, some more cactus and dust?"

"No, Kyle, but I think it needs another cow over there for balance." I pointed to the area I had in mind.

Kyle stood back and squinted. "Yeah, I think so too."

I located a cotton hand towel, dipped it in hot soapy water and scrubbed out Alicia's drawing of Father

Serra. I used a pencil and the Wild West book of pictures to draw the gambling scene onto painting location number three. Once the back wall, bar, table and chairs were painted in, I would add four poker players and a dance hall girl in her low-cut finery— something for the older-gentlemen frappé customers to ogle.

After five hours of painting, Kyle was finished with his dust-choked cattle-drive picture, and mine had a bar and bartender in the upper background area. I would build the picture back-to-front, ending with highlights in the dance hall girl's shiny black hair.

Alonzo fetched Breana from her class in Salinas at four o'clock, paid Kyle for his work at five and was serving happy-hour customers as Breana and I walked outside to my truck.

"Thank you, Josephine, for doin' what you did for me today," Breana said. "Nate kept askin' me about the sapphire ring all the way to Salinas. I didn't tell him what you told me, but he certainly put the pressure on. I can't figure Nate, you see. Sometimes he plays the lamb and sometimes he's a wolf, like today."

"I think Alonzo will keep Nate away from you," I said, trying to look confident. "But if all else fails, I'll hand over the ring. After all, his mother probably inherits it anyway."

"And you're a keepin' the ring because…?"

"Because I don't know if there really *was* a sapphire and if there *is* one, who has it, the killer? In my mind, the ring and the killer are linked like rocky and road. Sorry, that's an ice cream joke." There I go, thinking about ice cream again, I scolded myself.

"What if Henry, bless his soul, was killed for some other reason?" Breana said.

I confessed that I'd never considered another scenario, but promised I'd give it some thought. I waved goodbye to Breana and pointed my truck to the grassy hills of Prunedale. David had called me earlier in the day promising to bring pizza to the Trippy house around seven. He sounded pretty chipper on the phone after a routine dental appointment. His dental hygienist said she wanted to adopt one of his kittens. A second hygienist in the next cubical overheard the kitty conversation and asked if she could adopt a kitten too.

Roaring up the Trippy drive, I pressed the garage door opener and cruised into the building, stopping next to the Tesla. I walked through the house, checking to make sure no one had trashed it while I was gone. Everything looked to be in order. But something about the house phone caught my eye. The phone was in its dock, which sat on the kitchen counter, partially covering Lois' lists of *do's* and *don'ts*, contacts and itinerary. But I'd set the phone away from the paperwork. As I stared at the phone, it rang. I jumped.

"Hello."

"Hi, Jo, it's me, Alicia."

"Sorry, my mind was miles away."

"At David's house?"

"No—just thinking about Henry's death and the blue ring. I spend a lotta time thinking, for all the good it does. I'm also wondering if I moved the phone, or did someone else?"

"You're thinking someone has been in the house?"

"Not really—no big deal. How are you feeling, Allie?"

"That's what I'm calling about. I had my best day yet, even made lunch for the boys, left-handed, of course. I just wanted you to know so that you can quit worrying about me."

"What, *me* worry?" We both laughed. "Good, that means you'll be back to work for our October mural project at the Aromas Library?"

"Absolutely, I wouldn't miss it."

We hung up.

"Squawk!"

"Poor Boris, you always have to have the last word."

I went outside and tossed a tennis ball to Solow on the freshly cut lawn. Willy liked the game too. His rules included butting the opponent and the ball-thrower whenever possible.

Roscoe stayed on the sidelines, crowing and flapping his wings in the excitement.

Solow dropped the ball and barked.

I heard the doorbell ring, ran through the house and opened the front door.

David held a large pizza box with two rolled-up newspapers on top.

"So you're the paper boy," I chuckled as he moved through the house to the kitchen.

"What in Sam Hill?" Boris squawked.

"It's not for you, Boris." David set the box on the kitchen table. "Josie, it looks like you haven't read the paper in a couple of days. I think you'll be interested in Tuesday's edition." He opened the paper and laid it on the table.

"Oh, my God! That's me and that stupid Louden creep!" I felt my face go from simmer to red hot. "Why didn't you tell me about this?"

"I thought you'd take it a little better with a good dose of pizza."

"You know, it wasn't what it looks like. Yes, I smacked him with my purse, but he wouldn't give the ring back to me. I asked him nicely, twice. He just turned and walked away. This picture from the security camera doesn't really look like me, does it? How did you know it was me?"

"Actually, I didn't know for sure until now."

Chapter Thirteen

It was the morning after. After what? You might ask. Let's just say the after-glow of David's visit lasted through the night and was still with me Thursday morning. Not to mention his information regarding Stilts. Even noises like Roscoe crowing and Boris gagging couldn't ruin my good mood.

"What was that?" I said, as I leaped out of bed and stumbled down the hall to the kitchen. "What's going on, Boris?"

Boris lay on his back on the newspapers at the bottom of his cage, legs in the air, gagging.

"Oh no, Boris! Don't die. Lois will kill me!" I opened the cage door and bent down over Boris for a better look. I pried his beak open with my fingernails and looked down his throat. A little pink something was visible so I pinched it with my fingernails and pulled, hoping it wasn't part of his tongue. Out came a thin slice of pepperoni. I dropped the slice of meat on the floor outside the cage where Boris couldn't reach it.

I heard something behind me and turned around in time to see Solow swipe the pepperoni and devour it. It was the law of the jungle—*no waste*.

"Boris, talk to me." I never thought I would say that!

The big bird flapped around until he had his legs under him.

"Boris wants a cracker."

"Coming right up," I said from the pantry, feeling more than happy to give him anything he wanted. When

I came back with a cracker, Big Bird was looking in control of his world, sidling along his favorite perch, chattering like an over-caffeinated auctioneer. Once his mouth was full of cracker, I turned to *my* basic need—a cup of coffee. Mr. Coffee worked his magic while I showered and dressed.

I devoured a yogurt-strawberry shake and a slice of cold pizza while talking to Breana on the phone. She was a good listener and knew more than anyone else about Henry's murder case. She said she was eating her breakfast, so we munched and talked and munched.

I told Breana about David's visit with Stilts—the retired attorney living in Aromas. David told me he'd had a hunch the lawyer might have known Henry, but it turned out Stilts did not know Henry, but he did know Henrietta and her real identity.

"I don't understand, Josephine, why would she tell the attorney?"

"She had to if she wanted her will to be legal. David didn't get to see it, but Stilts verified the fact that a will exists. I guess I should pass that information on to Elvira."

"Indeed, of course, you must."

"Bree, do you have classes today?"

"Yes, and driving me to my class, Alonzo is, says he has business in Salinas."

"I think he wants to keep you safe from Nate's charms," I said.

She agreed and we hung up.

I finished my morning feed-the-boys routine and took off for San Juan Bautista in my trusty truck. At the bottom of the Trippy driveway, I looked left and right and left again. There was an old red Chevy truck parked in the grass and two guys wearing hats and sunglasses pretending not to see me. I rolled my eyes and pulled onto Langley, glancing at my rearview mirror in time to see the red truck turn right and disappear up the Trippy driveway.

They weren't following me, so what were Allen and Marvin up to? I felt compelled to turn around and find out. They seemed harmless enough, but their behavior was very peculiar. I drove slowly up to the house and parked beside the brothers' empty truck. I sat for a moment, staring at the wide open front door. The lawn had been mowed, carpets cleaned, what were they here for?

I climbed out of my truck, leaving the door ajar, and quietly stole past the gnome village, rose bushes, hydrangeas and on into the house.

I heard voices coming from the kitchen.

"Boris wants a cracker."

"Hey, Boris, you be quiet now!"

"Squawk!"

"Marv, it don't do no good to talk to a dumb bird."

"Hey, Al, look…." He pointed to me as I entered the kitchen. "Ah, hey there, Josephine!" Marvin quickly put a hand behind his back.

"Are you boys fixing the phone? I didn't know it was broken." The phone lay on the counter in two pieces.

"Actually, we ah…Al, you tell 'er."

"Tell 'er what? That we're puttin' somethin' in the phone?" Allen wiped his forehead with a rag from his pocket.

"What are you putting in the phone?" I asked.

Marvin pulled his fist out and dropped a tiny piece of metal on the counter. His eyes stared at the floor. He cleared his throat. "We don't know what it is, but we get paid to put it in the phone."

"I know what it is…." Allen said.

"Quiet, you idiot," Marvin hissed.

"Quiet, you idiot!" Boris screeched.

"Who are you guys working for?" I demanded.

Allen's chin dropped, his eyes focused on his boots.

"On second thought, you go ahead and put that little thing in the phone, that way you won't get into trouble. And don't tell anyone I saw you," I said, watching their facial muscles relax.

I watched Marvin quickly install the little listening device and then snap the two pieces of phone back together.

"One thing, guys, you need to hand over the house key." I held my hand out. "You can mow the lawn without a key to the house."

"Yes, ma'am," they said in unison as Allen dropped a key into my hand.

"And you didn't see me today...."

"Huh? I mean, yeah, we didn't see you," Allen said, as they turned and walked through the house. Truck doors slammed. The old Chevy engine sputtered and growled. Pointy red hats vanished under a smelly blue haze wafting across Gnomeland as the truck disappeared down the hill.

During my encounter with the brothers, an idea had hatched in my mind. I would talk to my friends on the phone about the blue ring, and see who might be listening. Then, I'd arrange a surprise for the trespasser. But in the meantime, I needed to get to work at the Crazy Horse. When I arrived there, Alonzo had just gotten back from Salinas and offered to carry my ladder into the building. I strapped a full canvas bag over my shoulder and carried a tarp and paint box into the saloon.

As I stood in the doorway letting my eyes adjust to the dim light, a feeling like butterfly wings touched the back of my neck. I turned and looked, but no one was there. I carried my bulky load between various tables set up for the lunch hour.

At the west wall, I stretched the tarp on the floor in front of the bar scene painting and prepared my palette. Several changes and details to the bar and bartender were rendered before lunch. By one o'clock, my muscles felt locked in place, my feet frozen on the third rung of the ladder, and my stomach growled.

I dropped my brush into the water bucket and took a stroll up the sidewalk, drawn to the smell of fresh bread and cinnamon rolls. But on my way to the bakery, I peeked through the jewelry store window. I saw Julia behind the counter talking on the phone, so I walked inside.

Julia abruptly ended the call. "Josephine, nice to see you!"

"I needed a break. How's business?"

"I don't know how Sam makes a living here. You're the first customer today, and you're not really a customer, are you?"

"No, just passing through," I lamented. "Have you heard anything from Rotsider?"

"That was him on the phone. I was happy to tell him a customer just walked in. He said he was waiting for a train outside of Paris. He's trying to get to Brussels."

"How about that? Lois is scheduled to arrive in Munich tomorrow, and Brussels on Monday. Small world."

"Yes, it is," Julia agreed.

"I follow her itinerary, imagining I'm there."

"I've traveled all over Europe. It was fun but I was so glad to come home to California," Julia smiled. "Have you had lunch?"

"No...what would you recommend?"

"El Jardine's. Shall we?"

"By all means."

The bell tinkled as Julia closed and locked the door behind us. With great will power, we passed up the bakery and walked two more blocks to El Jardine's. Since it was a lovely day in September, we asked for a table outside. The traditional Mexican food was very good, and the lush gardens all around us were another reason to love the place.

"Josephine, you look like you're a million miles away."

"Sorry, I was just thinking about something that happened this morning...."

"Really? It must have been exciting." Julia raised an eyebrow.

"I guess I can tell you, since you already know about the blue ring. The local handyman brothers have a key to the house I'm taking care of. It was quite a shock to find them in the house this morning, installing a listening device in the house phone."

"That's terrible! Did you call 911?"

"No, you have to understand, these guys wouldn't hurt anyone. They take odd jobs to earn money. Since they'd been in the Trippys' house many times before, maybe they thought it was okay to go in unannounced. As far as taking the phone apart, they must have known something wasn't right about that. But I just couldn't get mad at them because I'm sure someone else put them up to it. I did make them give back the house key."

"I'm glad you got the key back. Who do you think wants to listen to your phone calls ... and why?"

"I wish I knew. I have a list of possibilities, but the short list lives next door, and it's probably all about the blue ring."

"But who would want a blue-glass ring?"

"Someone who doesn't know about the glass part."

"Wow, are you sure you're safe in that house?"

"Oh, sure. Waiter, check please."

The waiter pulled a handful of checks from his pocket and gave me one.

Julia offered to pay. We settled for going Dutch and headed back to our work.

A couple of dozen customers were talking and eating when I walked into the saloon. The table nearest my painting hosted six *red hat* women wearing bibs, enjoying saucy ribs and sweet potato fries.

As I painted the bar scene, I felt alone without Kyle. I also felt like I was the entertainment *du jour* as I painted a wooden chair for the first poker player to sit on. The angle was all wrong. I painted out the chair and tried again. After one more try, I decided to take a walk upstairs for a fresh view of the painting from the staircase.

Halfway up the stairs, I stopped and stood against the railing to let two women pass on their way down to the dining room. A well-dressed woman thanked me as she passed. Feeling a chill, I waited for the second person, but when I looked up, no one was there. Was I losing my mind?

Alonzo charged up the stairs, looked at me and said, "Did you see her?"

"See who?"

"I guess you didn't," he mumbled and continued up to the landing and into his office.

When I finally took a moment to concentrate on my painting, I discovered it looked exactly the way I had intended. By the end of the day, I had created a rough tough cowboy, wearing chaps over jeans and a red-knotted scarf over his long-sleeved shirt, sitting on the chair. Three more chairs, three more poker players and a dance hall girl yet to be painted.

The lunchers had cleared out and happy hour would begin soon—my cue to go home. I decided to go to *my* house first, collect the mail and water the marigolds. I drove through Aromas and turned onto Otis. What a beautiful street it was, or did I just feel that way because David lived there? I passed by his property and then drove up my driveway. What a darling little house, adorned with window boxes full of marigolds, their little heads down, shriveled, leaves curled.

One thing was missing. Solow. He was the heart and soul of my home. I gave the flower boxes a squirt of water from the hose, unlocked the door and entered. Across the living room a red light blinked. My old-fashioned message machine had collected five messages. I found paper and pen and ran through each one.

One call was from Lois reminding me that her garbage cans should be placed at the bottom of the driveway every Friday morning for pick-up. Even after two weeks, the cans were only half full. I was in no hurry.

Another call was from Alicia. Maybe she'd forgotten Lois' number, and the call from Mom sounded like she just woke up and hadn't sorted things out yet, like where I was staying. My note pad stayed empty—no need to return any calls.

I pulled a package of frozen steaks out of the freezer, gathered up a few of Solow's favorite toys and two summer outfits from my closet. I stuffed everything onto the passenger seat of my truck and proceeded to the end of the driveway where I pulled about twenty pieces of mail out of the mailbox. I tossed all of it onto the front seat to be sorted later.

As I rolled through the neighborhood, I couldn't help turning up David's driveway. I wanted to tell him my plan, but should I tell him? I turned my head and there he was at my window. I rolled it down.

"Hey, beautiful."

"Hi, David, I just came by to collect the mail and stuff like that. Did you hear from Alicia?" He shook his head. "She wants us to come over for dinner tomorrow night. She said she's feeling better."

"That's good. About dinner, I think I can make it. I volunteered to mow a few fields in the neighborhood tomorrow, but I should be finished in time."

"Is my place on your list?"

"Naturally," he laughed. "Did you know you have paint on your nose?"

"Thanks for telling me. Would you like to stay with me Sunday night?"

"Huh? I mean, sure," he stammered. "I never thought you'd ask."

I looked in the rear view and rubbed at my nose with a tissue. "It's not what you think. I'll explain later. I gotta go feed the boys now; see you at six tomorrow?" He nodded as I backed down the driveway, cranked the truck to the right and proceeded down Otis wearing a sizable grin on my face.

I made the trip to Prunedale re-running David's shocked expression when I asked him to stay over night with me, arriving at the Trippy house still smiling. But once I walked into the kitchen, I gave my full attention to Boris. I planned to spend some quality time with the bird and even more time with Solow.

"Hi, Boris, how ya doin?"

"Stuff it."

"Is that a nice thing to say...?"

"Boris wants a cracker."

"Okay, coming up." I handed him a cracker, topped off his food and water and went outside to take care of my other three boys. Solow galloped over to me, but Willy got to me first since his legs were longer. They danced and hopped around while Roscoe crowed from a safe distance.

"What in the world?" I moaned when I caught sight of something floating in the pool. When the boys finally settled down, I was able to take a closer look at the debris. Lois' flowering red geranium plant and a wooden windmill from the gnome village bobbed along the edge of the pool. A trail of dirt ran across the sidewalk from the pool to the gnome garden near the back gate.

Solow hung his head in shame while Willy bounced around like an over-inflated basketball. By the time I'd scooped the stuff out of the pool with a net and swept the concrete, it was way past my dinner time, heading into evening snack time.

Solow followed me into the house. I quickly threw together a bologna-croissant sandwich which we shared, followed by ice cream and later a big bowl of popcorn. We watched reruns and a few minutes of the eleven o'clock news. Next thing I knew, it was three a.m. I heard something, stood up and took the half empty bowl of popcorn to the kitchen.

"A message?" I said to myself in the dim light from the kitchen appliances.

"Back up now!" Boris croaked.

I jumped. "You don't scare me, Boris." I said as I pushed the message button.

"Josephine, it's Lois. Tom's ulcer is acting up, and he didn't pack his medicine. Could you please look on the top shelf of the bathroom cabinet, the one with a mirror, and tell me if his prescription is for Anaprox or Aciphex?"

I played the message again and wrote down the two drug choices on a slip of paper. I felt my way through the house to the master bathroom and turned on the light, giving my eyes a good shock. There was no mirrored cabinet with shelves inside, just wide mirrors and countertops full of perfume bottles, exotic soaps and the ubiquitous crystal gnome collection. I scratched my head. Not a masculine product in sight. I checked the bedroom walk-in closet and found nothing but Lois' dresses, suits, slacks and sweaters.

By that time, Solow was up, tail wagging like it might be time for breakfast. He trotted down the hall with me to the next bedroom. I flipped on the light. The bed cover sported a red and brown Indian design with matching pillows. I peeked into the closet—all men's suits, pants and shirts. I counted zero gnomes.

The Indian bedroom had an attached bathroom. I turned on the lights. This manly room was a bit smaller than the master bath, and not one single gnome lived in here. I opened a mirrored cabinet above the sink and spotted a bottle of medicine on the top shelf. I held the bottle in the light and read the label.

Poor Tom must have been in pain. I went to the kitchen immediately and called Lois. She answered on the second ring. I told her the name of the medicine.

"Thank you, Josephine. Tom has been sick most of the trip."

"That's too bad. Do you have a doctor to prescribe this stuff for him?"

"We hope to find one today. Everything okay at the house?"

"Everything is fine, no worries." I said and hung up.

"Hands up!" Boris squawked.

"Stuff it, Boris." My nerves were on life-support. I turned the lights out and trundled off to bed.

Chapter Fourteen

Friday morning finally arrived after a fitful try at sleep. I had tossed and turned for hours, wondering if Tom and Lois never had children because they had separate bedrooms. Maybe Tom snored or Lois talked in her sleep. What did it matter? They were old and deserved to live anyway they wished. The real question was what would *I* be doing at their age, twenty-five years from now?

I pondered those same questions as I painted the bar scene at the Crazy Horse.

"Top ah the mornin' to yah, Josephine," Breana beamed and walked up to the painting for a better look.

"Same to you, Bree. Going to class?"

"No classes on Friday," she smiled.

Alonzo thundered down the stairs, hooked his arm into hers and together they left the restaurant.

I managed to paint a round oak table and two more chairs into the bar scene. I thought about going to the stairs for a fresh look at the painting, but shivered when I remembered the weird feeling from the day before, like someone was standing next to me. What I needed was lunch and someone to talk to, so I headed over to the Jewelry Company. Julia saw me coming and met me at the door, key in hand. She locked the door even before I asked if she wanted to go to lunch.

The bakery drew us in like hornets to a barbeque. We ordered the perfect lunch—ham and cheese on a freshly baked croissant and iced ginger tea. After a few bites, we relaxed and talked to each other like old friends. I learned that Julia was currently living in Hollister with her three cats. She'd been married and then divorced. Her children were grown and had moved away.

"Any news from Mr. Rotsider?" I asked.

"Thankfully, no. Did I tell you that I'm taking care of his dog while he's away?" She pursed her lips.

"No, you didn't. Is that a problem?"

"The dog sheds. Everything I have is covered with long white hair. I vacuum everyday, but it's no use. I'm beginning to think the old man went to Europe to get away from his deaf and blind old dog." She rolled her eyes and brushed a few hairs off her tan slacks.

"I hope you get extra pay for all this inconvenience," I said.

"I'm working off a present for my mother, a diamond necklace. She's turning eighty in November and I can't wait to give it to her. By the way, have you had any more break-ins?"

"Nope."

We paid our bill and walked back to the jewelry shop. Julia unlocked the door and stepped inside. I was right behind her.

"Julia, do you sell many watch batteries?"

"Yes, we do…."

"Are any of them five-hundred dollars?"

"Ah, wow! I don't think so…unless it was a special order. I've only been here two weeks and there's a lot I don't know about the business yet."

"Would it be possible for me to look at receipts from July of this year?"

Julia cocked her head. "I guess so, why?"

"Just curious about a battery sold July 13th of this year."

Julia went to the back room and returned with a folder marked *July*. I opened the folder and flipped through a batch of pink receipts. I found one from July 13, an identical twin to the yellow carbon copy I found in the Tesla.

"Thanks, Julia, unfortunately this doesn't tell me anything new." I showed her the copy.

"Who buys a watch battery for five-hundred dollars?" Julia said, shaking her head slowly.

"The Trippys. Thanks, Julia, see you later," I said as the door tinkled and I stepped outside. Breana and Alonzo had just arrived at the Crazy Horse. I followed them into the building, still thinking about the five-hundred-dollar battery.

My first glance at the painting in progress told me I needed to paint a mustache on the cowboy to make him look older. From there I worked on the fourth chair and a bottle of whiskey on the table.

Friday's happy hour began at four-thirty with the arrival of a local bike club, giving me an excuse to leave early. I packed up the truck and managed to pull into traffic without knocking over a single Harley Davidson motorcycle. I headed to Prunedale for a shower and a change of clothes, planning to look and smell good for David.

As I cruised up Langley, I decided to check on Henry's place. I pulled to a stop behind Elvira's truck, cut the engine and walked up to the front door. Before I rang the bell, I peeked through the window. There was Elvira, her mouth open, eyes closed, body stretched out and hanging over the end of Henry's Lazyboy. She looked so comfy I almost hated to ring the bell. I rang it three times before she opened the door.

"Josephine, where'd you come from…I mean, what time is it anyway?"

"It's almost five. I just stopped by to see if you need anything."

"Right. And my mother was married to the Pope," she snarked.

"Really, I just want to help out since you're new in town."

She rolled her eyes and led me into the house.

I sat on the arm of the sofa, ready to flee if necessary. I heard a crunch under my derriere and moved onto the left cushion of the very old camel-back loveseat. From there, I looked at the dirty dishes on the dining room table—two place settings and two coffee mugs.

"You want to know if Nate is living here with me, right?"

"I think he is, but so what?"

"Well, doggonit, he's my son! Of course, he's stayin' here." Elvira folded her arms over her ample belly as her eyes dared me to disagree with anything she said.

"Elvira, I'll get right to the point. I have good news for you. Stilts, I mean, Mr. Forman, handled your Grandmother's will…."

"Well, thank yah, darlin' for that piece of information. I have been lookin' everywhere around the house."

"This house has been searched more times than you would believe. Even the Trippy house has been tossed," I said, sighing with disgust.

"If this is all about the will, why would anyone look for it at the Trippys' place?"

"I think they were looking for something described in the will…a sapphire ring, maybe?"

"I can believe that!" Elvira folded her hands in her lap and leaned forward. "I already told you that that ring is the last piece of Henry and Grandma's treasure." She gave me a hard stare, practically daring me to flinch.

I felt my face heating up and decided to leave. I stood up to go.

"You can find Mr. Forman in the yellow pages," I added. My boyfriend, David knows Mr. Forman through the Eagles. He says the man is retired and lives in Aromas."

Elvira followed me out to the porch.

"Let me know how it turns out," I said. I handed her my business card, climbed into my truck and drove up to the Trippys' house.

The boarding house for bad boys was chaos as usual. When all the water and food bowls were filled and piles of poop scooped up and the concrete hosed off, I treated myself to a hot shower. As I toweled off, I heard the kitchen phone ring. I wrapped a big blue towel around my body and ran down the hall to pick up the phone.

"Hello?"

"Hi, Josephine, it's Lois. How are things going?" I detected insecurity or distrust in Lois' voice. Was she worried about her house?

"Fine, everything is just fine here. It must be midnight where you are."

"Yes, it is midnight...I couldn't sleep."

"That's too bad. What can I do for you?"

"So nothing unusual has happened....?"

"Huh, no...nothing unless you saw my picture in the paper," I laughed and rolled my eyes. If only she knew how embarrassing *that* was.

"To tell you the truth, my friend Clair put a picture from the *Sentinel* on Facebook. I wasn't sure it was you until now. Why did you hit the man with your purse?"

Oh boy, she thinks a crazy lady is taking care of her house.

"It was like this; I handed the man a ring and he wouldn't give it back. I asked twice and he just kept walking. I was kinda' messed up from the storm drain and both knees were skinned, tangled hair, stuff like that. I guess he thought I was homeless and stole the ring."

"Henry's ring?"

"How did you know?"

"Everyone knows you have it."

"Don't worry. The ring is safe in your sugar bowl."

"Oh, my," she giggled and hung up.

Suddenly I felt weak. What had I said about the ring? Was anyone listening in? How many people knew I had it? I made a mental note to be more careful with my words in the future as I sat on the edge of the tub, blow-drying my hair, my body still wrapped in a towel.

I sensed I wasn't alone and looked up. There was David standing in the doorway, wearing a baby blue button-down shirt tucked into Levis. His smile said so many things, most of them cause for me to blush. I asked him to bring in the Trippys' mail and newspaper. Lois had asked me if they should stop the paper for a month but I'd said no, I would like to read it. I didn't say I definitely would have time to read it, but at least I'd be able to look at it now and then when I had the time.

David just grinned at my request and stood his ground. Between the dryer and his manliness, perspiration ran down my back and tickled my bum. He leaned down and smelled my hair. That seemed to satisfy him for the moment. He turned and left the room. A couple of minutes later, talking through the closed bathroom door, he stood in the hall asking where he should put the mail.

We chatted about all kinds of things through the door while I styled my hair, darkened my eyelashes with mascara and reddened my lips. I hooked silver loop earrings into my ears and slipped on a pair of jewel-studded black flip flops to go with my black pants and white tunic. I checked the mirror and turned out the light.

David found me in the hall. We embraced. One thing led to another. Half an hour later, we were worried we were going to be late for dinner at Alicia's. I quickly ran a brush through my hair, applied more lipstick, grabbed my purse and we took off in David's Miata.

Squinting behind our sunglasses, we rode toward a big red sun wishing the ball of fire would hurry up and drop into the Pacific Ocean. Watsonville and Alicia's house were welcome sights. Even better was seeing Alicia not wearing a sling. Her hand and arm were a bit puffy still, but she was able to use them, gently. However, a new symptom became obvious as the evening progressed—a twitch here, a twitch there. Her various parts were twitching without her permission or control. A foot, an elbow, a finger, an eyebrow, they moved on their own. Obviously, the spider's poison had made its way into Alicia's nervous system.

At first, David and I acted like nothing was going on. But when Alicia's hand twitched right in the middle of eating blackberry pie, I couldn't hold it in. Alicia thought it was funny too, and then we were all laughing as she wiped pie off her cheek with a napkin. Trigger was the last to join in—not wanting to disrespect his mother. Once he got started, he howled like Solow. His dog, Tansey, began howling her little-dog howl under the table. We laughed until our sides hurt. Two weeks of tension and feelings of guilt fell away like icicles in sunshine.

Ernie, David, Trigger and Tansey went to the back deck to look at Trigger's bug collection.

Alicia and I cleared the table. As I passed by the dining room window, I saw a faded red truck parked across the street. In the dim evening light, two baseball caps and one droopy mustache gave the brothers away. They were at it again, following me and snooping into my life.

"What's the matter, Jo?" Alicia asked.

"See that old red truck over there—the Chevy with two dorky guys in it?"

"Okay, do you know them?"

"Those are the guys I found in the Trippys' house taking the kitchen phone apart. It was in pieces and they were about to install a listening device. I decided to let them go ahead and bug the phone, that way I can get information to whoever's been after the blue ring. In fact, I have a plan. I'm going to call you tomorrow and tell you where the ring is hidden and mention the fact that I'll be going out on a date with David Sunday night. What I won't say is that our date will be at the Trippys' house, waiting for an intruder."

"I'm glad you included David in your plan. Since when does he approve of your sleuthing and such?"

"I just asked him to stay with me Sunday evening. He said he'd be happy to."

"So you didn't tell him everything...."

"I'll tell him when it's time. I'm not ready yet...."

David walked up and put an arm across my shoulders.

"Ready for what, Josie?"

"Ah, for an oil change—my truck is due."

David and I rinsed the dishes and loaded them into the dishwasher, giving Ernie a chance to relax and read the paper while Alicia read a chapter of *Tom Sawyer* to Trigger. For a second, I almost felt like an old married person, and it felt good. David must have read my mind. With his hands still in the sink, he leaned my way and kissed my cheek.

The next time I looked out the dining room window, the streetlights were on, giving the Chevy truck and the brothers a yellowish luster.

After the usual goodbyes and hugs, David walked me out to his Miata.

The brothers slunk down even further into their seats.

"David, it's been ages since you let me drive. Do you mind?" I said as I opened the door to the driver's seat.

"What madam wishes, madam gets." He smiled, handed over the key and helped me into my seat. I revved the engine, waiting for David to shut his door. I hit the gas and we took off with a squeal.

David adjusted his seatbelt.

"Wow, I forgot how fast this thing goes," I giggled. I made a tight circle at the end of the block, roared down to the main street, turned right on College and right again on East Lake, one of many ways to get to Aromas. But I wasn't going to Aromas; I was trying to lose two goofy guys in a pickup. At the intersection, a yellow light went red and we jerked to a stop. The truck caught up to us just as the light turned green.

I decided to play a little cat and mouse game with the boys. I kept my speed down so the boys could keep up with us. I turned onto the steep and narrow Highway 152 heading east, better known as *Hecker Pass* or *how the heck do I get off this road?* The Miata charged up the mountain, hugging the turns like a muscle car on a race track. After a few miles of not seeing the boys in the rearview, I pulled into a private driveway and turned off the lights.

The old Chevy chugged past us, up the road and around the bend.

I clicked the lights on and cruised down the mountain into Watsonville.

"What was all that about?" David asked.

"Some guys I know were following us. They'll be in Gilroy soon," I laughed.

"If that old truck makes it," he said. "What guys are we talking about?"

"I told you about the handyman brothers. It seems they're spying on me, or someone has put them up to it—not sure what's going on yet. They bugged the Trippys' kitchen phone and every time I turn around, there they are, pretending not to be watching me.

"Are we talking about the red pickup that was parked across the street from the Quintana house?"

"See, they can't even hide from you. Those fools could use some lessons in spying," I laughed as I drove up the Trippy driveway and shut the engine down. We clambered out of the car and stood close in the dark under a billion stars enjoying whiffs of jasmine and a hint of barbeque smoke riding on a soft breeze—heaven on earth.

The roar of an engine and a flash of light moved up the hill and around the oak tree, stopping in front of the Trippys' front door. Car doors slammed. Officers Lund and Sayer walked closer to us, back-lit by their vehicle's headlights. With mega flashlights in hand, they asked permission to go inside.

"Can David go home now?" I asked.

Sayer nodded his head and said it would be okay for him to go.

David shook his head, indicating he wasn't ready to go home.

I unlocked the door and the four of us went inside. I flipped on the lights and we settled into the comfy sofas.

"Would anyone like a soft drink?" I asked, trying to cut through the official, sterile atmosphere. "What can I do for you?"

"Ms. Stuart, it has come to our attention that you are in possession of a certain sapphire ring. What do you have to say?" Lund asked, chin up, lips puckered, slits for eyes.

"Yes, I have the ring. I found it in Willy's poo."

"Who or what is Willy?" she asked, looking like she'd just swallowed a fly.

"He's a little baby goat. Willy belonged to Henry and the silly goat accidentally ate the ring. I found it, cleaned it up and took it to a jeweler in San Juan Bautista to see if it was real. Mr. Rotsider said it was real gold, very old, but the stone was glass. I decided to get a second opinion. A jeweler in Santa Cruz said the ring used to have a sapphire and was very old."

"You kept the ring even though it didn't belong to you...." Lund snarked.

"I kept the ring safe because Lois was in charge of Henry's property, but she's in Europe. As a house sitter, it was up to me to take care of Henry's animals *and* the ring until the will is read. And there *is* a will. I just found out about it." I could hardly wait until it was read and the burden of responsibility lifted off my shoulders. I looked to see how David was taking all this news.

He winked at me. "Josephine is telling you the truth," David said. "Actually, she's been taking care of the Trippys' property and Henry's place because I asked her to. Originally, I promised my friends I'd do it...."

"Thank you, Mr. Galaz. We believe Ms. Stuart," Officer Sayer said. "We'll take the ring now, Ms. Stuart."

I walked into the kitchen and flipped a light on.

"What in Sam Hill?" Boris squawked.

I dug into the sugar bowl with my fingers, pulled out the ring and rinsed it off under the tap. I dried it with my shirttail and took it directly to Officer Sayer.

"What happens to it now?" I asked.

"We file it until we hear from the legal claimant," he said.

"Have you found the murderer?"

"We have a person of interest."

"Is it Samuel Rotsider?"

"No, why do you mention Mr. Rotsider?"

"Just throwing out names," I shrugged.

Sayer wrote the name into his notebook, reached in his pocket and pulled out a small clear-plastic bag with a button inside it. He held it out to me.

"It's just an ordinary shirt button. It was found at the Hobblestone crime scene, but it didn't match anything on the victim or anything in her closet. If you know where this button came from, please let us know."

I took a good look at the plain white button with four holes in the center and promised I'd call if I found out anything new. But my mind was on the ring. Even before the officers drove away, I felt a sense of loss. It seemed the old ring had had a hold on me. We'd been through a lot together. I reminded myself that the ring would look better on Elvira's finger than at the bottom of a sugar bowl.

My concerns about the ring continued into my dreams that night. I woke up at four a.m., sweaty, heart racing. I remembered being buried in a giant sugar bowl with sugar up to my nostrils and more granules pouring onto my head, threatening my ability to breathe. Just when I thought all was lost, Solow pushed the bowl over on its side. It broke into a dozen pieces. I crawled away from the mess with a big blue ring around my middle toe.

Chapter Fifteen

First thing Saturday morning, still under the sheets, I curled my body into a knot and felt my feet toe by toe. Thankfully, I didn't find a big old ring on one toe. I opened my eyes, hoping to shake the recent nightmare that felt so real.

A wide-awake nightmare of a bird squawking and ranting, along with a dog barking and a few cock-a-doodle-doos, reverberated through the house. I finally gave up and trudged down the hall to see what the commotion was about.

I found Solow outside, jumping up and down, barking at the back door to be let in. *What the heck is going on?* I wondered. I didn't remember leaving him outside. In fact, I remembered him falling asleep in his doggie bed while I memorized every minute of my evening with David before falling asleep. *How did Solow get outside?* I scratched my head, let my poor basset in, poured kibble in his bowl and put the coffee on.

"Boris wants a cracker."

"Okay, Boris, coming right up."

Boris had worked through a whole box of saltines, so I opened a box of graham crackers and gave him one. He held it with one foot, pecking at it with obvious distain. But in the end, he ate the cracker. If only he could tell me how Solow got outside. I looked around the kitchen. Something didn't look right, but I couldn't put my finger on it. So out of habit, I looked to see if the ring was safe.

"Oh, no, the sugar bowl is gone!" I groaned. "It was right here last night." Was I going crazy? Was I losing my mind? Alicia was a good judge of character and always nurturing and kind when it came to my idiosyncrasies and misadventures. I picked up the kitchen phone and dialed my best friend. Alicia answered on the sixth ring.

"Jo, calm down. I can't understand a word you're saying."

"Like I said, the sugar bowl—the hiding place for the ring—is missing. Someone has been in this house! They even put Solow outside. I don't know why I'm being careful with my words now. The crooks already stole the sugar bowl. Hear that, crooks? You stole a stupid sugar bowl! What am I going to do, Allie?"

"Take it easy, Jo. Call the police. They'll know what to do."

"They were already here last night, and I gave them the ring! Did you hear that, crooks? I gave the ring to a deputy sheriff!" I took a comforting sip of coffee.

"So you're worried about more break-ins?"

"No, I guess not. But it galls me that someone can break the law and invade my privacy." Not to mention scaring the bajeezus out of me!"

"You're just mad because you slept through it," Alicia laughed.

"Okay, I guess I feel better. Thanks, Allie, for listening. I gotta get ready for work now." We hung up. I looked around the kitchen and made a mental note to clean house as soon as I had some time. I finished breakfast and the usual feed-the-animal chores, stacked more dirty dishes into the sink and headed my truck south to San Juan Bautista.

I parked at the curb directly in front of the Crazy Horse since all spaces were empty. The whole town was quiet as dust. I pounded on the door several times.

Finally, the door opened. Alonzo stood in the doorway
wearing Levis, bare feet and a sleepy smile. He blinked
his eyes as sunshine streamed in the door, landing on
tight Latin skin over muscle. I barely noticed his
incredible physique.

"Hi, Josephine, is it ten already?"

"It's ten-fifteen but who's counting?"

He stepped aside as I hauled a six-foot ladder
through the dining room. For once, Alonzo didn't help
me unload the truck. He excused himself and
scampered up the stairs to his room to finish dressing. I
heard two doors close upstairs.

I was happy to have the dining room to myself for a
change, no one at the bar commenting on what color the
horse should be or whether I should add more thorns to
the cacti or paint a rattlesnake in the picture. Now that I
was painting a bar scene, they had all kinds of ideas,
like paint a rattlesnake under the table. How original!

I had painted quite a bit by one o'clock, including a
cowboy sitting at the table with one hand on the
whiskey bottle and his cards fanned in the other hand.
His plaid shirt took more time than anything else. When
his rolled-up sleeves were finally finished, I painted a
brown leather vest over the shirt and added an empty
holster at his waist.

Alonzo opened the restaurant for lunch at twelve
and Breana waited tables. She seemed to know what
she was doing and the customers liked her, especially
one old geezer who gave her a pat on the butt.

"Mother of God! Keep those hands to yourself old
man! You're quite mad and not intended to be after the
likes of me," she laughed and sashayed across the room
to a table of four women waiting to order.

I needed to stretch my legs, so I crossed the street
and walked several blocks up a hill to the mission,
making a quick tour through the old stables, admiring

the ancient buggies and carriages. From there, I cut across the lawn and passed through the mission's rose garden and back down to the street.

A few minutes later, I arrived at the bakery. Julia stood at the counter. She turned when she heard my voice.

"Julia, this proves that great minds think alike."

"Hi, Josephine; I checked the Crazy Horse but you weren't there. My nephew said you went out to get some lunch."

"Yep, and here I am." We ordered the Saturday special, ham and cheese on a poppy seed bun, and carried our little bakery bags to a cast iron bench on a patch of grass two blocks down the street.

"Josephine, have you ever wired money?"

"No. Sounds like something they do in the movies."

"I need to wire money to Mr. Rotsider. It seems his wallet was stolen at the airport in Brussels. He said he needs three thousand dollars to get to Antwerp. He needs hotel and food money, but he still has his plane ticket home. He said he plans to be in Antwerp until the twenty-fourth."

"So what's the problem?"

"Mr. Rotsider gave me the address of a hotel in Jeete, outside Brussels, where he's staying until he can take the train to Antwerp. I've never sent money before. He told me to go online and use Western Union. But first, I'm supposed to take three thousand dollars from his cash register and put it in a bank account in my name. Then I use that account number and send the money to him."

"I guess that's reasonable," I said, wondering if I'd do something like that for my employer. What if Lois needed money? Would I go to the trouble to send it? Of course, I would.

"The thing is we haven't had much business lately. We're a couple of hundred dollars short of three thousand. I tried to tell Mr. Rotsider over the phone, but he was already hyperventilating over the fact that he'd been robbed. I don't blame him for being upset."

"I wouldn't trust him if I were you," I mumbled.

"What was that you said, Josephine? You wouldn't trust him. Why not?"

"Just between you and me…there's a possibility…a very slight possibility, that he stole the sapphire from the blue ring. You know, the ring I brought in…the one he took his time dealing with…the one he said was only glass."

"You don't mean that."

"It's a hard accusation to make because whoever has the sapphire is probably the person who killed Henry."

"Oh, dear!" Julia's face lost all its color.

"If I were you, I'd send him all the money in the register, minus a hundred dollars for the till. It's plenty of money for a first-class stay in Antwerp, I'd think. Just pretend like nothing's wrong. When he gets back, we'll see what the police think. Maybe he's not the one."

"Now you think he's not the one…make up your mind, Josephine."

"I wish I could. It might be Nate or his mother or Marvin and Allen or Stilts…."

"Do you suspect me?" Julia asked.

"Of course not, but you did clean the ring…but no, I don't think you did it."

"Well, that's good," she laughed. "Who's Stilts?"

"Henry…etta's lawyer, and the only person who knows who the beneficiaries are and what they'll inherit." I made another mental note to visit Mr. Forman.

"Josephine, just one more question—where can I find a bank that's open on Saturday afternoons?"

I didn't know the answer to Julia's question. I'd already said too much, and it was time to get back to work. Since I was the owner of Wildbrush Mural Company, there was no one to boss me around, no timecard to punch, no one to see that I was punctual except me. As we walked down the street toward our work, I wished Julia good luck finding a bank. She laughed and said she'd drop in to see the murals when she had time. She unlocked the shop and stepped inside.

I continued down the block to the Crazy Horse. The cavernous dining room echoed country music and conversations from two tables of Saturday afternoon diners, the only ones left from lunch.

Breana had already dished out their bills and shed her little apron full of pockets. She'd climbed onto a bar stool next to Alonzo and was sipping iced tea. He said something in her ear and she giggled.

I painted for another three hours. After the first hour, I decided to give myself a break from the poker table. At the far right side of the painting, I added an old west, double-swinging door. Above and below the door, a street scene was revealed, including a mysterious shadow on the wooden walkway outside.

I thought I heard a chuckle and looked over my shoulder—no one there. I shivered as a chilly draft passed right through me. I checked to see if a window was open. They were all shut tight.

I painted parts of a cowboy—legs and boots below the door and eyes and a hat above the door. I stood back for a better look. The mystery man had eyes and eyebrows like Groucho Marx.

Alonzo stood behind me studying the painting. "The cowboy behind the door reminds me of someone."

"Groucho Marx?"

"No, I think his name is Pazzio; he plays the guitar," he said. "Looks just like him."

"Okay, that's who it is," I laughed. "Where's Breana?"

"She's upstairs getting ready to go to dinner and a movie with Julia, since I have to work tonight." He bit his lower lip, trying to garner some sympathy or a laugh.

It was almost five and three couples had already kicked off Saturday night happy hour. I quickly packed up my supplies and hustled everything out to the truck in two trips. As I brought the snug-top down, I heard a familiar voice.

"Josephine, I'm glad I caught you," Julia said. "Breana and I are going to dinner and a movie at the Green Valley Cinema tonight. Would you like to join us?"

I thought about the boys, my needy charges. "I'd love to go to a movie, but first I need to take care of things at home."

"Okay, Breana and I will have dinner at the Nifty Fifty and meet you at the theater at eight. See you there!" Julia said, and ducked into the Crazy Horse.

Back at the Trippy house, it was the same old chaos, translating into guilt on my part for not spending enough quality time with the guys. I grabbed a bag of peanuts from the pantry and shared them with Boris. I was starving, but Boris just wanted to talk. He jabbered on and on as I looked around the kitchen, finally realizing that it was spotlessly clean. My jaw dropped. How did that happen? Lois must have a cleaning woman I wasn't told about.

I gave Boris a few more peanuts and then went outside. The lawn was freshly cut and trimmed, everything in its place. Even the goat, chicken and dog poo had been disposed of. My job was easy, play ball with the boys. I pulled a soccer ball out of the pool house and rolled it to Solow, but Willy got there first and leaped over the ball into the pool.

Solow must have thought swimming was the next activity on the agenda and jumped in with a splash that soaked me from the knees down.

From out of nowhere, Roscoe flapped his wings down an imaginary runway and created a semi-successful take-off.

The moment Roscoe became airborne, I ran to the shed for pool equipment, namely the long pole with a net on the end. Knowing the bird's limitations, I carried the pole to the edge of the pool closest to Roscoe's flight pattern, keeping an eye on Solow and Willy as they paddled toward the stairs at the shallow end.

As predicted, Roscoe hit the drink half way across the pool. I made several tries at netting the obstinate bird and finally hauled him out of the water. He looked small and ridiculous, but his pride was intact as I dumped him onto the lawn. The haughty little man-bird strutted across the grass, flapped his wings and jumped onto the barbeque and from there up to his perch on top of the pool house.

I dropped the pole and ran down to the shallow end of the pool where concrete stairs could be seen through the water's surface. I stood knee-deep on the second step encouraging Solow to keep coming. Finally, his paws found me. He scrambled out of the pool with a push and a lift from behind.

Mr. Wild and Crazy was still swimming in every direction with no signs of saving himself. I called to Willy, pleaded with him and finally left the pool to get the pole-net. I lugged the pole to the edge of the pool, and looked around...no Willy!

Bam! I took a bump to my thigh. There was Wet Willy at my feet, butting me for attention.

I dried Solow and then Willy with a holey beach towel from the pool house and made a mental note to buy new towels before Lois and Tom came home from their trip. They'd been gone fifteen days, which meant they had fifteen more days of Europe and I had fifteen more days with the boys. I fed everyone, grabbed a soda from the fridge and dropped onto a sofa. I clicked the remote and that was all I remembered until seven-thirty.

My eyes opened at the sound of a weather report video on TV of a tornado barreling toward a housing project in an eastern state.

"Oh, no; it's after seven." I shot out of the living room, down the hall and into the bedroom to change out of my paint clothes. A shower would have been nice, but it was already seven-thirty. I wriggled into some clean clothes and ran a brush through my hair. Knowing I'd be going out in the evening, I had left the truck parked near the front door. I climbed in and roared down the driveway with the setting sun in my eyes. I turned onto Langley. Two seconds later, I heard a terrible bang-crunch-scraping noise as my whole truck quivered.

I pulled off the road and cut the engine. My heart pounded as I ran on shaky legs around the truck and back toward Henry's mailbox. With tunnel vision, I pounded through a few yards of dry grass along the edge of the road. Near Henry's driveway, in front of the mailbox, was a lump of black metal, tires spinning, arms and legs splayed on the ground. I recognized the black helmet.

Without seeing a face, I knew immediately who was on the ground. I bent over Nate to see if he was breathing. He blinked his eyes open and looked up at me.

I jumped back.

"Sorry I hit you, Josephine."

I figured he was out of his mind. "No, I'm sorry I hit *you*," I said with what little voice I could muster. "Are you okay?" Silly question, but I didn't know what else to say. My mind bounced from blank to worried to scared and back to blank.

"Help me up, would ya?" Nate stretched an arm up.

I took his gloved hand and pulled. My legs shook like crazy, threatening to collapse. I tried again. Finally, I pulled him into a sitting position. He looked over at his motorcycle with tears in his eyes.

"Shall I call an ambulance?" I asked.

"No. I don't need this on my record." He stood up. "Let's get this bike over there behind the bushes for now." Precariously, he stood up, bent on moving his bike. He leaned down gingerly and pulled on a handlebar. I pushed on the other one until we raised the big old Harley enough to drag, push, and roll it across three yards of grass and drop it behind a patch of brush. From there, we walked over to my truck to see how it had taken the collision.

"A bit of a dent, some black paint...but not as bad as I expected," he said and dropped to the ground.

"Oh, no...what happened...are you all right?" My heart beat so hard I could hardly breathe.

"I'm just a little shaky and my ribs hurt. I guess you could take me to a doctor." Even in the dimming light, I could see that his color wasn't good.

"Should we let your mom know what happened?"

Nate shook his head. "She'll kill me," he said, as he leaned against my truck.

I opened the passenger door and supported his elbow, helping him onto the seat. Once he was in, his head dropped back, his eyes closed.

My phone rang.

I ignored it.

My thoughts were scary. What if there was internal bleeding? I rounded the truck and climbed in. Twenty minutes later, we were in Watsonville at the Doc-in-a-Box on Green Valley Road. It was eight-thirty and the place closed at nine, but a nice lady doctor agreed to take an x-ray and patch him up.

Nate came back to the waiting room with a bandage on his right elbow and another on the right side of his forehead.

We waited impatiently for chest and leg x-rays.

"I didn't see you coming, Josephine. I looked left and right and then I pulled out."

"I was in a hurry...." I said, feeling horribly guilty.

"It wasn't your fault, Josephine. When I finally saw you coming, I swerved to the right, but not fast enough." He relaxed as much as a large person in a small chair can.

My phone rang. I answered it.

"Breana, I'm sorry, I forgot to call you. There was an accident...."

"Mother of God, a smash up? Are you all right, Josephine?"

"Nate ran into my truck with his motorcycle. We're waiting for the doctor to tell us if he broke anything."

"And how's the motorcycle?"

"Didn't look good."

"Can I be speakin' with Nate?"

I handed the phone to him. He brightened a bit but his voice was pathetic. Obviously, he was looking for sympathy. He stood and walked to the other side of the room. After a long chat, he hung up and handed back the phone.

An hour ticked by. The doctor ushered us into a small examination room.

Around ten o'clock, the doctor came back ready to show us the x-rays. She fitted Nate with a Velcro walking boot for the right leg because he'd fractured a small bone in his foot. She told us that two ribs were cracked but would heal on their own. She taped his mid-section and prescribed pain pills.

The moon had crossed a good section of sky by the time we finally climbed into my truck. Nate's stomach growled. I was pretty hungry myself. He said he'd decided to ride to town for a burger just before he broadsided me. He offered to buy me a triple cheeseburger at a place down the road. We ordered at the take-out window and ate our million calories without leaving the truck. Nate's knees were in his chest and his head touched the roof, but he managed to put away two triple-decker cheeseburgers, three tacos and two buckets of French fries.

I had one turkey burger and a few of his fries. "Nate, how can you eat so much?"

"I'm only 22 years old. I can eat all I want," he laughed. "Ouch, it hurts to laugh."

"That's what you get for being young and crazy!" I laughed. "How's your mom?"

"Okay, but she's a terrible cook. I sneak out for fast food whenever I can."

"Nate, I know this is none of my business, but if you and your mom inherit Henry's house, will you guys live there?"

"No, we like Texas. We can't wait to get back home."

"Has Elvira talked to Stilts, I mean, Mr. Forman?"

"She has an appointment for Monday morning."

"Nate, how did it happen that you were the first to find the body?"

Nate stared straight ahead at the road, his jaw tight, probably debating whether to tell me everything or not.

"You know that I really dig Breana," he began. "Well, I went to the house that day to see her, but the door was open and she was gone. My grandmother was on the floor...as soon as I saw her, I knew she was dead, but I didn't know what to do so I called 911 and then my mom."

"Where was your mom?"

Mom and I were staying at a motel in Salinas and she drove right to the house. While I waited for the police, I looked around for any clues. I didn't know my grandmother very well, just three visits with her in my whole life, but I was very upset. I knew her enough to know that she'd never kill herself, and she wasn't stupid enough to do it accidentally."

"It must have been terrible for you."

Nate nodded and continued to unload his thoughts and feelings. "As much as I care for Breana, I thought maybe she'd pulled the trigger." Nate hung his head.

"What made you think that?"

"She's trying to work her way through school and Grandma had told Bree she's in the will."

"Wow, I don't know what to say...."

"While I was alone, waiting for the Sherriff, I cleaned everything with a rag and soapy water, the gun, the shells, everything. When the first two sheriffs arrived, I stepped on a button lying on the floor. Just an ordinary white button, like from a shirt...anyone's shirt. I had to give it to the officers because they were right there in the room with me. I wanted to hide it, but they saw me pick it up."

"Nate, I wouldn't be too worried about Breana. I can't imagine her murdering anyone."

Chapter Sixteen

My first phone call Sunday morning was from David. Even before he said a word, I knew he was calling about Sunday night. I had asked him to stay with me—no explanation why. Being of the male variety, he didn't need an explanation. David didn't know it, but he'd been a crucial part of my plan to catch a thief. But in two days time, everything had changed. The sheriff's deputies had the blue ring and the thief had already stolen Lois's sugar bowl. Who would be dumb enough to steal a sugar bowl? I scratched my head and answered the phone.

"Hi, David, I'm glad you called. I have big plans for us tonight."

"Really? I mean that's great. What time should I come over?"

"I thought we could barbeque about seven, and I have a great movie planned for later." David sounded happy with the plan, but I needed to come up with a good movie before the end of the day so I called Alicia.

Her message machine answered. I remembered that the family was probably still at church and would spend the afternoon at the soccer field. If I couldn't find a good home movie, maybe I could take David out to see the movie I'd missed the night before. I called Breana. She assured me the movie was nothing but a chic flick and not worth the effort.

I called Julia.

"Hi, Josephine, this is a surprise."

"Julia, I promised my boyfriend a good movie at home tonight, but I don't have one. Any ideas?"

"I'll ask Alonzo and get back to you."

"Were you able to send money to Mr. Rotsider?"

"Not yet; I couldn't find a bank open after four on a Saturday. I'll take care of it Monday. Poor Rotsider will have to eat beans for a couple of days. Talk to you soon, Josephine." We hung up.

I called Nate.

"Josephine, hello…I'm really sorry…."

"Never mind that; I need a good home movie to watch with my boyfriend tonight. Do you know of one?"

"Sure, got it right here. *The Godfather*… I know it's old, but he'll love it."

"I haven't seen it, but I don't know about David. I'll give it a try. Thanks, Nate."

"I'll be home all day," he grumped.

The phone rang.

"Hi, Julia, what did you find out?"

"Alonzo recommended *The Godfather*. Why are you laughing?"

"I already have a *Godfather* movie lined up. Thanks for getting back to me."

I no sooner put the phone down than it rang again. It was Mom.

"Hi, Mom, what's up?"

"Your father and I were just wondering if you had plans for dinner?"

"Well, just a backyard barbeque…."

"Mind if we come over? I have a lovely tri-tip. Bob tells me our barbeque is out of gas. I told him it would be a good chance to see this house full of animals you're always talking about."

"Okay; bring the meat around six. I told David we'd eat at seven."

"Oh, David, are you sure you want us there…?"

"I'm sure, Mom." We hung up. I was relieved to know that the main course was taken care of, but a little worried about how David would feel about company. But Mom and Dad were old. They'd go home early.

I let Solow and Willy out the back gate, and we gaily romped and slid our way down the hill in knee-high grass, all the way to Henry's house. Willy and Solow chased each other around the goat barn while I waited for Elvira to open the front door. I noticed Nate's motorcycle leaning against the barn.

I put my fist up to knock again.

The door lurched open. Elvira stepped back and asked me to come in.

I wondered if she'd kill me with her bare hands for driving into her son.

Laying on the sofa, propped up with pillows, a glass of juice and a bottle of calamine lotion in easy reach on a side table, Nate raised a blistered hand and smiled painfully—or pathetically—depending how you looked at his situation. Either he was in more pain than the night before or he was playing up his injuries. I had to admit he looked worse in the morning light, his face red and puffy, eyes watering.

Elvira's droopy eyes spelled *a hard night with little sleep*. I had to give her points for her obvious mothering skills. She pulled a chair from the corner of the room and positioned it between her recliner and the sofa.

My head swiveled right and left as Elvira and Nate took turns talking about his injuries from the accident plus a nasty rash of poison oak from the brush where he hid the motorcycle. Elvira explained to us how she'd managed to haul the Harley up a ramp into the bed of her truck at five o'clock in the morning, by herself!

Elvira offered me a cup of tea. She put the teakettle on the stove while I made myself comfortable at the kitchen table. The kettle whistled, she poured hot water into two of Henrietta's mugs, handed me a tea bag and held up a sugar bowl, asking if I wanted sugar.

"Oh, my God! Where did you—I mean—is that Henry's sugar bowl?"

"No, Henry and Henrietta never had a sugar bowl. They kept sugar cubes in that ugly mug on the windowsill."

"If you don't mind my asking, where did you get this sugar bowl?"

"I was fixin' some tea for the brothers and I offered them sugar from the old cracked mug. Allen said he had a sugar bowl he wanted to give me. Had it right outside in his truck. I thought that was real sweet of him. It even had sugar in it."

"I hate to tell you, Elvira, but that bowl was stolen from Lois' house."

"How do you know that?" She squeezed her eyes real skinny.

"You saw the bowl at the Trippy house! You even held it up to show me when I was looking all over for a sack of sugar. Don't you remember?"

"You're right, Josephine! Now I remember seeing it, but there's more than one of these two-handled thingies in the world," she grumped.

"The other part of this whole thing is that Lois' sugar bowl is missing." I waited for her to admit I was right.

"You can have it if you think it belongs to Lois," she said. "I don't even know the woman, but God knows I wouldn't take her sugar bowl."

"I really don't give a hoot about the bowl, Elvira, except that it's part of an expensive set of dishes. But I would like to have it back in the house by the end of the

184 *Scent of a $windle*

month, before Lois comes back from Europe. The *real* problem is that the brothers keep breaking into the Trippy house when no one's home. I *took* their key, but that didn't stop them from coming back. I think they have another key. They're probably at the hardware store right now having half a dozen keys made—just in case."

"They're not bad boys," Elvira said, "*men* actually, just a little slow on the uptake. I try to keep 'em busy doin' little jobs around the house." She took a sip of tea.

"Like bugging Lois' phone?"

"Huh? Oh that," she sputtered, sending tea drops across the table. "I already knew you had the ring...I just wanted to stay up on current events." Her cheeks flushed.

"Then you know that the Sheriff has the ring now and someone *else* has the sapphire...."

"*What* did you say?" Elvira's jaw dropped; her eyes flamed.

"Someone traded cut glass for the sapphire!" I took a sip of tea and watched her expression go from moderately friendly to shocked and confused. "I think whoever took the sapphire also killed your grandmother, but I'm short of certain on that point."

"Josephine, I can hardly believe what you're sayin'." She gulped some air and let it out slowly. "Does the sheriff know who dun it?"

"I don't think so, but they're working on it. At least, Officer Sayer says they are." I took a last sip of tea and told Elvira I needed to get back to Lois' house.

Nate gave me the movie and some quick instructions on how to play it. I didn't listen carefully because David would know how to do it, which reminded me I needed potatoes and onions for potato salad.

I stepped outside and called the boys. They hopped and skipped with excitement, churning up driveway dust. Eventually, they fell in line and followed me back to the Trippy house. I was breathing hard as I opened the gate and walked past gnometown. Solow peed on the mayor and Willy danced around the mayor's wife, knocking her flat. Three little gnomes smiled at us as we marched across the lawn. Solow and I went into the house, leaving Willy outside to dance with the gnomes.

I closed the back door.

"What in Sam Hill?"

"Hi, Boris, how are you today?"

"Boris wants a cracker."

I rolled my eyes. "Tell me something new. We'll see you later, old boy." We went to the garage. I loaded Solow into the truck and we rode to my favorite Watsonville market. I loved spending quality time with my favorite four-legged guy, the only one who liked me to sing-a-long with music from the radio. Solow howled randomly, adding the bass to our impromptu duet.

I parked about twenty yards from the store under a shade tree, rolled the windows to half mast and trotted over to the store entrance, passing by a familiar green Volvo station wagon with a soccer sticker on the back bumper. Expecting to see Ernie somewhere in the building, I was surprised to see Alicia pinching avocados in the produce section.

"Hi, Allie, where's Ernie?"

She turned and smiled. "I left Ernie and Trigger at the soccer game. I drove myself to the store," she beamed. "It feels good to feel good." One eye twitched and then her lower lip. She laughed. "A few little twitches aren't a big deal."

"It's good to see you back in the swing of things."

"I'm so glad to be able to drive again. Help me find a soft avocado, Jo."

I helped her paw through a large pile of rock-hard green avocados. Suddenly, I looked up and realized my friend Robert was watching us.

"Ladies, can I help you?"

"I'm making guacamole and I need one more ripe...."

"I'll check the stock room. Sometimes we have over-ripe avocados that we toss." While Robert was in the warehouse, we kept our search going. He returned with four large black avocados.

"You are awesome, Robert!" She kissed him on the cheek.

"I'll ring you up when you're ready—those are free." He pointed to the ripe avocados Alicia put in her cart.

"Are there any more back there?" I asked.

"Yeah, at least four more. I'll get them." He came back with five big black avocados.

"Looks like I'm making guacamole tonight. That would go well with tri-tip, don't you think?"

Robert said he thought they went together and suggested I make a strawberry short cake for dessert. He even picked out three little boxes of berries for my inspection. I placed the boxes in the cart and grabbed a ready-made white cake and a carton of whipping cream. Alicia and I combed the aisles for corn chips, olives, pickles, milk, bread and unsalted sunflower seeds for Boris.

"Jo, looks like you're doing some serious cooking tonight," Alicia said.

"I am. Why don't you and Ernie and Trigger come over for dinner about seven?"

"That sounds great. Can I bring something?" she asked.

"No, not really; I think I have everything." I took a quick inventory of the contents of the cart for the tenth time in ten minutes.

"I can't wait to see the Trippy house and all the animals," Alicia giggled.

It was about time I had the Quintanas over for dinner since I ate at their house almost every Friday of the year. But what was David going to think? No more intimate dinner party for us. I silently promised myself I'd make it up to him another time.

We pushed our baskets up to Robert's check stand.

Alicia went first. The bagger carried her bags to her car.

Robert, never known to be coy, talked about his landlord, his cat and his niece and nephew. The seven-year-old twins had been a handful of trouble when he took them for a train ride through the forest at Roaring Camp in Felton. When the train stopped at the top of the mountain, the kids slipped away from Robert. A search party made up of train passengers, one engineer and one hapless uncle finally found the children halfway up a pine tree a quarter mile from the railroad tracks.

"What are you doing tonight, Robert?"

"I get off work at six. I'll probably grab a burger on the way home."

"That's all? How about coming over to Prunedale for dinner?"

"Prunedale? You don't live in Prunedale."

"No, but I'm house sitting there." I wrote the address on the back of my business card and handed it to him. "Bring a bathing suit."

"Okay and I'll bring a bottle of wine," Robert said with a big smile. "I turned twenty-one last week." He bagged my groceries and carried them to the truck. He spent a few minutes talking to Solow and gave him an ear rub. I was glad Robert could come to dinner. I always enjoyed his company even though I was almost thirty years his senior. Besides, I owed him a great deal for all the helpful pointers he'd given me in the last couple of years.

I arrived at the Trippy home a little after two. Boris squawked when I opened the garage door into the kitchen. He watched me closely as I unloaded and put away four sacks of groceries. When that was done, I put a pot of potatoes and a pot of eggs on the stove. While they boiled, I checked on the boys outside.

Willy and Solow frolicked around the pool as if they hadn't seen each other in ages. Roscoe chased the two rascals, hopping and flapping across the lawn and through gnome town. Solow stopped to pee on a pointy red hat while Willy chewed on Lois' lovely nasturtiums.

I scooped poop off the concrete and washed it down with the hose.

Suddenly, I remembered the stove. I dashed into the house and pulled the pots off the burners. Fearfully, I pulled off the lids. Ninety percent of the water was gone in both pots, but nothing had burned. I stabbed a potato with a knife and it fell apart, stem to stern into mush. I filled the egg pot with cold water, hoping they'd survived.

For the next three hours, I worked in the kitchen making iced tea, various salads and the dessert. I cleaned the kitchen and set the dining room table with Lois' good china. I picked flowers and created a centerpiece. Next, I made myself presentable in an ankle-length wrap-around black skirt, a white peasant blouse and the large hoop earrings Mom had given me. I stood back and looked in the mirror to see if I'd forgotten anything.

The doorbell rang.

I opened the door expecting to see Mom and Dad, even though it was a bit early.

"Bree, Alonzo...."

"Hi, Jo, I hope you don't think us completely mad. We just stopped by to see the little fellow, Willy himself, if ya don't mind. Alonzo has never met the dear boy," she laughed.

We moved through the house to the backyard where the three boys had crashed on the lawn for a nap. They heard us and came back to life, dancing around with new energy and cock-a-doodle-do's.

The doorbell rang and I excused myself to go answer it.

I opened the door. "Hi, Mom, Dad." We hugged, unloaded the car and carried the tri-tip, Mom's banana bread and a big green salad to the kitchen. Mom wore her red sari and Dad looked comfortable in shorts and a polo shirt.

"Back up now!" Boris squawked. "Hands up!"

"Oh, my, he's a bit nasty, don't you think?" Mom said, stepping back from the cage.

"Full of bluster," Dad said, stepping closer to the big bird.

"He's not so bad, once you get used to him." I put the salad in the fridge and we migrated to the backyard. I introduced Breana and Alonzo to my parents.

"What a lovely name, Breana. Are you staying for the barbeque?"

"I, ah...."

"I was just about to ask if you and Alonzo would like to join us for dinner," I said.

Breana looked at Alonzo. He gave her a nod and I suddenly had two more dinner guests.

The doorbell rang.

I left the group, ran through the house and opened the front door. There was Trigger with little Tansey in his arms. The Quintanas poured into the house just as Robert drove his car around the oak tree and parked. I watched him open the back door, lean in and unfasten a couple of seatbelts. A little redheaded girl and a tow-headed boy leaped out of the car, ran to the oak tree and tried to climb it. Robert followed and pulled them away, crushing the petunias at the base of the tree. The seven-year-old twins followed him to the door where I stood, biting my lip.

"Josephine, this is my niece, Molly, and her brother, Mick. My sister unexpectedly needed some help tonight," he shrugged.

"Nice to meet you, ma'am," they said in unison as they took off through the house with Robert close behind.

I heard a familiar engine-roar coming up the drive. A second later, David's Miata appeared. He found a spot to park and moseyed up to me looking like he'd arrived at the wrong house. We embraced. I took my time, not looking forward to facing the explosion of guests, and inevitable questions from my boyfriend about our dinner date.

Finally, I pulled away and led David through the house to the large gathering of people in the backyard. Fortunately, Lois and Tom had plenty of lawn furniture and space for children to run—in this case, run after Solow, Tansey and Willy…and one terrified chicken.

I introduced David to Alonzo.

"Nice to meet you," Alonzo said. "What's the occasion?"

I stepped closer and put my arm across David's back. "We're celebrating our tenth anniversary of being friends," I grinned. Would David buy it? Did he keep track of such things? In truth, we'd only known each other nine and a half years.

The crowd bought it, clapping and smiling.

David turned and kissed me in front of everyone. For a moment, it felt like we were engaged, but I wasn't ready for that.

Dad had already taken charge of the barbeque.

Mom placed a loaf of garlic bread wrapped in foil at the back of the barbie on the upper slow-warming level.

Ernie joined Dad at the barbeque and Mom and Alicia went to the kitchen to work on side dishes, leaving me free to watch chaos in the form of three children, three animals, one chicken and a swimming pool. The twins stripped their clothes off and ran around in bathing suits.

Alonzo had his iPod with him and proceeded to crank up the volume, sharing his favorite boleros and rancheras. David and I began moving to the music. Pretty soon we were dancing around the patio. Breana and Alonzo joined us, whirling at twice our speed. We laughed and danced to the music until exhaustion slowed us down to a waltz. Bree and Alonzo didn't have that problem; they just kept going until Alonzo tripped over little Tansey and fell into the pool, taking Breana with him.

I ran into the house and brought back a couple of towels. When I returned to the pool, Molly and Mick had decided it was okay to swim and Robert waded in to keep them from drowning. It turned out that Robert didn't know how to swim and the twins were future Olympic material. They swam in the deep end with Trigger while Robert stood on the stairs at the shallow end of the pool, worrying like a mother hen.

Mom and Alicia came outside to watch the fun.

Ernie took Alicia by the arm and whirled her around the patio.

Not to be out done, Dad tagged Mom and off they went.

Bree and Alonzo were drenched and giggling but back for another dance.

David grabbed me and off we went, feet moving to the beat. I laughed until I cried.

When black smoke poured out of the barbecue and floated over the patio, everyone turned to see what was burning. Dad flipped the barbeque cover open and flames shot forward. He stepped back.

Ernie reached in and shut things down but the fire continued to burn. He grabbed a flaming loaf of bread with a pair of tongs and tossed it onto the lawn where it burned itself out.

Mom looked down at the black foil and shook her head.

"The good news is, the meat is just fine!" Dad chirped. He loaded the tri-tip onto a plate and took it to the kitchen. Mom followed him inside, reminding him where he went wrong with the bread.

I took Breana to my room and gave her some of my clothes to change into. She joined us at the dining room table looking like a little girl wearing her mother's clothes. I told her I'd launder her wet skirt and blouse and get them back to her. Alonzo liked the way she looked in the over-sized clothing, but it was easy to see that he liked her no matter what she wore.

The twins, Trigger, Alonzo and Robert had towels wrapped around their wet clothes. By the time they'd finished dessert, they were shivering and ready to go home. Everyone left by nine o'clock except David. That was when the second party started, the one with two people, a little music, some wine and, "Who let the goat in the house?" I said as David took off chasing the little devil through the living room where he'd been eating the leaves off a fake potted plant.

After an evening of goat chasing, kitchen cleanup and lots of lovin,' it was time for us to part. I walked

David to his car. The crisp air and radiant moonlight made it hard to say goodbye.

I watched the Miata's taillights disappear down the hill.

Exhausted and ready to go to bed, I removed Breana's damp clothes from my bed and tossed them in the laundry basket.

I crawled under the covers and said goodnight to Solow who was already snoring in his doggie bed, all partied-out!

Chapter Seventeen

I woke up Monday morning feeling like a stranger in my own life. Since when did I throw big parties and dance all night? Just having little children around was unusual. But throw in two dogs and a goat, and this was someone else's life. I'd always tried to keep a certain order in my life—no unexpected diversions from the norm. But through it all, the only part of the party I regretted was the mushy potato salad with rubbery eggs and too much mustard. Sadly, Mom knew it was her recipe I'd mangled.

Solow gave me a lick on the cheek as if to say, "Enough lying around, let's get up and eat breakfast." My thoughts exactly. We tramped down the hall and I opened the blinds letting in the morning light.

Boris didn't react. He just slept, clutching his perch with his talons.

"Hello, Boris. Does big bird want a cracker?"

Boris slept on.

"What's with you, Boris? Time to get up, old boy."

Solow barked.

Boris slept.

I let Solow outside, and went back to pestering Boris. "What is *that* doing inside the cage?" I said to myself. At the bottom of the cage, next to Boris' teacup was an empty wine glass. I remembered Mick messing around the cage, and Robert pulling him back to the dining room to finish his dinner. Robert didn't have a moment's rest the whole evening.

I let Boris sleep it off, put Mr. Coffee to work and trundled down the hall for a leisurely shower. My preliminary plan for the day was catch up on housework and laundry, spend time by the pool working on a tan and rest up for Tuesday.

Showered and dressed, I made a breakfast omelet using two eggs, leftover bits of tri-tip, chopped tomato, and onion and cheese in the middle.

"Boorriss waants a quaackerrr." His body swayed side to side as his eyes rolled up to the ceiling and his topknot flared at an angle.

I put my fork down and walked up to the cage.

"You are in bad shape, old boy." I gave him a cracker. He nibbled one corner and let the rest drop to the floor. I checked his water and food dispensers and was shocked to find gummy bears in his sunflower seed cup. Not only was he schnockered from wine but he was full of sugar. I dumped the bears and filled the cup with fresh seeds.

I went back to my omelet, saving a piece of it for Solow. As I ate, I flipped through the phone book looking up S. Forman, I found about fifty Formans; but only one had attorney at law behind the name. I dialed.

"Hello, Mr. Forman...."

"Yes, this is he...."

"My name is Josephine Stuart and I'm calling you about a sapphire ring."

"Yes, I believe I know the one, Ms. Stuart. I can see you at two o'clock." He hung up.

What if two o'clock didn't work for me? Who did he think he was...but I'd be there, of course—how else could I ask questions that had nagged me for so long?

I threw a load of dirty clothes in the washing machine and filled the dishwasher with dishes from the night before. The grungy tile floor needed mopping, but I decided to ignore it and let the housekeeper take care of it, along with the white carpets sprinkled with crushed corn chips, pickle pieces and gummy bears.

I let Solow in and gave him the remains of my omelet.

One gulp, no chewing, gone!

We walked outside. I inspected the backyard, dreading all the things I'd have to clean up from the party. I took the gnome family, one-by-one, down from the bench swing and set them on the ground where they belonged in Gnomeland. I threw the burnt foil-covered bread into the garbage can along with six empty cans of cream soda. No wonder the kids were hyperactive. I pulled debris out of the pool with the net, swept the concrete and washed everything down with the hose.

Except for the kitchen floor and carpet messes, the Trippy house looked pretty good. At a quarter to two, I drove to Aromas, took a right on Carr and another right on Pointer Park Drive. I found number 3250, a lovely peaked-roof house sitting a hundred yards back from Pointer with a view of the eastern foothills. I parked next to an older black Beamer, climbed the half dozen stairs to the front door and knocked.

The door opened. A very tall, wrinkled gentleman asked if I was Josephine and invited me to come inside.

"Mr. Stilts…I mean, Mr. Forman, I'm taking care of Henry Hobblestone's property because the Trippys are in Europe. I'm house sitting for them…."

"Yes, I know the situation. A friend of yours was here this morning. Elvira is very concerned about Henrietta's ring." His hawkish eyes drilled into me.

"As you probably know, the sapphire has been replaced with glass," I said.

Stilts nodded politely and waited for me to continue.

"I found the ring in goat poo—but that's another story. I washed the ring and took it to a jeweler in San

Juan Batista, Mr. Rotsider, who took his sweet time examining it. Three days to look at a stupid ring. I should have known he was up to something. My question to you is, if he really did switch the stones, am I responsible?"

"Hum, difficult to say."

"Evidently, Mr. Rotsider knew Henry for years. Maybe he killed Henry for the ring, but couldn't find it because it was hidden in a sack of oats. And then I came along and handed over the ring. I feel just awful!"

"Have you asked Mr. Rotsider about the missing stone?"

"No, by the time I found out about the sapphire, he was on his way to Europe."

"What part of Europe?" His thick eyebrows twitched with interest.

"Antwerp."

"Antwerp? Interesting," he mumbled.

"Why is that interesting?"

"This week there is *Minerant*, an international gem show in Antwerp, but that could be a coincidence...."

"I don't believe in coincidences."

Stilts rubbed his boney chin. "Neither do I. You might want to contact your local law enforcement and tell them what you just told me."

"You're right, Mr. Forman. I've been putting off the inevitable. I appreciate your advice." When I stood up to go, Mr. Forman checked his watch.

"Normally, I charge by the half-hour but it's only been eighteen minutes so we'll forget it this time," he smiled.

I had no idea he might charge me, and felt grateful he hadn't. I thanked the attorney for his advice; we shook hands and I walked down the stairs to my truck. I stood in the sunshine for a moment observing a massive fog bank crawling my way between the hills like a fluffy white monster, swallowing everything in its path.

Two miles away, my home sat on the western side of the Aromas hills, where ocean breezes kept the fog away, but not always. I drove up Otis and parked near my sweet little adobe. I pulled mail from the mailbox and checked the answering machine for messages.

I finally left Aromas and drove to Prunedale where the milky fog was moving inland, forking its way up the canyons, obliterating the landscape along Langley Gulch Road. Even the gnomes could not be seen from Lois' kitchen window.

Solow and Willy bounded around the pool paying no attention to the weather.

Fair Weather Roscoe preferred to hunker down in the pool house.

I pulled Officer Sayer's card out of my purse and punched in the numbers. I told him I had new evidence. Sayer said he and Lund were working a case in Salinas and would be over to see me later in the afternoon around five.

Next, I called Julia at the Jewelry Company.

"Josephine, nice of you to call on your day off."

"Julia, are you going to be in the shop for the next hour?"

"Sure, I'll be here. What's going on?"

"I'll tell you when I get there." I quickly locked up the house and drove to San Juan Bautista. After weeks of working at the Crazy Horse, I could drive the route in my sleep. I yawned, wishing I had a cup of coffee. I curbed the truck in front of the bakery, ordered two coffees and carried them down the street to the Jewelry Company. The door tinkled and Julia looked up from the Bart Gilbertson mystery novel she was reading.

"Working hard, I see."

"I know you're not here for a watch battery," she chuckled.

"You're right, but there *is* something I need. Would it be okay if we looked through some files?" I had second thoughts about invading Rotsider's privacy, but I reassured myself that he had nothing to worry about if he'd done nothing wrong.

Julia looked around the shop. "I guess we could. What are we looking for?"

Without answering, I circled the long display counter and entered a small backroom with a granite-topped workbench, gem-cutting equipment, microscope, scales and such. Light filtered through one small, barred window on the west wall. I flipped on a fluorescent light and examined a bookshelf along the north wall, beside the door. Large gemology books monopolized the two lower shelves. About a hundred or so manila folders filled the top shelf.

Julia pointed to the folders. "Each one represents a month of receipts."

"I'm not sure what month we want so let's start with May." I pulled down a folder tagged May of the current year, laid it on the workbench and opened it.

Julia leaned over my shoulder.

I searched through dozens of receipts from May. Nothing. I continued the search month-by-month all the way to September and found nothing but ordinary jewelry business. I was just about to give up when I noticed a row of drawers along the side of the granite-topped workbench. I pulled out the top drawer and right on top of a pile of miscellaneous papers was a brochure. Not just any brochure, but one advertising the Minerant. My heart beat faster. I opened the colorful pamphlet, wondering where the jeweler had obtained it and when.

Julia moved closer for a look. "Josephine, it says the Minerant is in Antwerp...and starts tomorrow! Do you think Mr. Rotsider will go to the show?"

"Does Willy have horns? Yeah, I'm pretty sure he will," I growled. Of course, he's going there. The Minerant would be the perfect place to find a buyer for the stolen sapphire. I shoved the brochure into my purse. Stilts was right. Unfortunately, the show started Tuesday. Maybe it was already Tuesday in Antwerp. I felt a trickle of sweat run down my spine.

"Josephine, what's the matter?"

"I think your boss is trying to sell Henry's sapphire. Can you find a magnifying glass for me?"

She dashed to the main room and came back with a looking glass.

While Julia was gone, I pulled down the July folder and found the Trippys' receipt. I laid it out on the workbench under lamplight and used the magnification to examine Rotsider's scribbles. I read *watch battery* and *Bezel Ring cleaning.*

"Julia, what is a Bezel Ring?"

"Let's look on the internet," she said, leading me back to the main room and an iPad behind the counter. She turned it on and quickly found Bezel Rings. They were pocket rings from the Renaissance period, typically topped with a diamond, sapphire or emerald, and used to carry perfume, snuff or poison.

"That's it!" I slapped my forehead. "He switched the stone in July, two months before I found the ring in the goat poo. It happened when Lois brought it in for Henry to have it cleaned. That's when Rotsider made the switch."

Julia, slack-jawed and shaking her head, just stared at me.

"Sounds like my career in the jewelry business will be short."

"Sorry, Julia, I have to go. The sheriff will be at my house…soon.…" I hurried past our cold coffees that we'd left on the glass top of the showcase and was out the door, dashing to my truck. I turned the key and sped off to Prunedale. No need for caffeine. My heart was racing along with my imagination. In my mind I could see old Rotsider showing the blue stone to potential buyers in Antwerp—or did he already have a contact person?

My truck roared up the driveway and into the garage.

As I stepped into the kitchen, I heard the doorbell ring.

"Hands up!" Boris ordered.

"Stuff it, Boris." I ran for the front door and opened it.

"Ms. Stuart," Officer Lund began. "We *should* be giving you a driving ticket.…"

Officer Sayer stood behind her. "We were following you through Prunedale, trying to keep up." He faked a frown. "Now, what is this new information you have for us?"

"Come in, and I'll tell you." I asked them to sit down while I went to my purse in the kitchen. I came back with the brochure.

Lund was looking at corn chips and gummy bears on white carpet, her mouth pruned in disgust.

I opened the brochure and handed it to Officer Sayer. "This is Minerant."

"And what is a Minerant?" Officer Lund asked.

"It's the name of an annual gem show in Antwerp, and Mr. Rotsider is there right now with the missing sapphire." The words tumbled out of my mouth like gumballs from a vending machine. But the officers weren't catching all the balls.

"You mentioned Mr. Rotsider once before," Sayer remarked.

"He owns the Jewelry Company in San Juan Bautista where I took Henry's ring. I wanted to know if it was real...you know, an antique, real gold, that sort of thing. Today I took another look at a receipt I'd found and discovered that he switched blue glass for the sapphire two months ago, and now he's in Antwerp probably selling the stone for millions!" I took a breath.

"That's quite a leap, Ms. Stuart," Lund said. "Where did you get the brochure?"

"I got it from a friend who works at the Jewelry Company. It was just lying around and she said I could keep it."

Lund looked right through me. "May we see this so-called receipt?"

I pretended not to notice her intense stare. "I'll get it for you." I hurried back from the kitchen with the receipt and handed it to Officer Lund.

She glanced at the piece of paper. "Terrible handwriting; our guys will take a closer look at this."

"I think it's a huge coincidence that Mr. Rotsider has the stone," I said, "He's in Antwerp and this Minerant brochure was in his shop. He might have killed Henry for the ring because he did tell me that he'd admired the ring for years and knew it was very old."

Sayer nodded his head sagely and Lund looked a little less like she wanted to lock me up and throw away the key.

"Because the stolen sapphire was taken to Belgium," I said, "does that mean the FBI will get involved?"

"We don't have an answer to that question at the moment, Ms. Stuart. Thank you for coming to us with this information," Officer Sayer said. "Please let us know if you learn anything new." He stood up and followed Officer Lund out the door.

Finally, the house was quiet, except for Boris talking to himself in the kitchen.

Being female, living alone and having a bunch of new information floating around in my head, I dialed my friends. First, I spoke to Alicia, then Mom, Briana and finally David. By the time I got to David, I was already in bed. I never knew how he would react to things in my life such as murder and robbery. He usually leaned toward "mind your own business, Josie," and "let the law take care of it." But lately he'd been much more tolerant of my snooping activities.

"Hi Josie, I tried to call you today, guess you were busy."

"Yeah, guess I was. I had a little visit with your friend, Stilts. He warned me about the Minerant."

There was a long silence. "Okay, what's a Minerant?"

I explained everything to David—how I believed that Rotsider had stolen the sapphire and taken it to Antwerp. My sweetheart barely objected to anything I said, maybe because the killer/robber was overseas and physically away from my curiosity and me. We talked until we were both yawning. Since I had to paint the next day, I finally said, "Goodnight." We hung up.

I left the phone on the nightstand.

The Minerant followed me into my dreams. I found myself in a giant gold-plated ballroom dancing with Mr. Rotsider. He wore a black tux, a large pocket watch and pink bunny ears. I saw a lump in his breast pocket and tried to put my fingers around it. When I was finally able to pull the lump from his pocket, it turned out to be a piece of coal.

People were stationed in booths around the room, selling rocks to gentlefolk.

Lois and Tom twirled by in their finery, making ugly faces at me just because I was wearing Levi cut-offs and a tank top. More and more people left their jewelry displays and appeared on the dance floor.

I looked around the crowded dance floor and noticed the Trippys were gone. Through a giant arched doorway, I saw Tom fall into an outdoor pond full of alligators. I had a feeling someone pushed him.

Suddenly, I was at the edge of the pond. Someone pushed me. I tried to scream.

Solow put his nose on my cheek.

I opened my eyes.

Chapter Eighteen

My cell phone did a dramatic rendition of Beethoven's Fifth.

I slapped it.

A moment later, when I was fully awake, I picked up the phone and answered.

"You sound a little grumpy, Josephine…."

"Lois? Why did you call me on my cell?"

"Because you didn't answer the house phone."

I looked over at the clock. "It's five-thirty here…."

"I'm sorry about that, but I only have a few minutes before I board the train. I just wanted to check in with you, and see if the house is okay. Did anyone call for me? Anything new?"

"Everything is just peachy. No one has called you…where are you now?" *No calls at all. Didn't she have any friends?*

"I'm catching a train to Antwerp…." A thundering train approached, making conversation impossible.

I hung up and dropped off to sleep, the phone still in my hand.

At eight o'clock, the phone rocked me out of a sweet dream about David as the mayor of Gnomeland and I as his fair maiden.

I answered the phone. It was Alonzo letting me know that I could come in to work early if I wanted to, since his day had started early. I told him I'd be in at the usual time, ten o'clock.

I climbed out of bed and stretched.

Solow walked with me to the kitchen. I let him outside and started the coffee brewing.

"Boris wants a...."

"I know what Boris wants." I grabbed a cracker and poked it through the wire cage.

"Hands up, squawk."

I laughed at Boris' antics all the way to the laundry room. He liked to show off by hanging upside-down from his perch. With both arms, I scooped a pile of clothes from the dryer and carried them to my bedroom for sorting and folding. Breana's cute little white shirt and her beige and white-checked skirt went into a separate pile. Too bad the cotton button-down blouse was missing a button. I bagged the clothing and made a metal note to drop it off at the Crazy Horse.

"Oh, no!" I pulled the white blouse out of the bag and inspected it. Moaning, I realized the four-hole missing button was the same size and type as the one Officer Sayer had shown me. Maybe the button had fallen off when she was cleaning Henry's house. I hoped with all my heart that Breana was not the murderer but mulled over the possibility as I drove to work.

Tuesday morning at the saloon was quiet...empty, actually. I gave Breana's bag of clothes to Alonzo to give to her.

"Is something wrong, Josephine?" he asked, taking the bag.

"No, nothing, really. Is everything okay with you and Bree?"

"Yeah, perfect," he smiled.

I painted most of another cowboy/poker player until one o'clock and decided to see if Julia would join me for lunch. As soon as the shop door opened and the bell tinkled, she hooked her purse on one shoulder and we headed over to the bakery for the Tuesday special, corned beef on freshly baked rye bread. We sat at a tiny metal table outside the building near the front door.

"Alonzo told me about your party," Julia mumbled as she worked on her sandwich.

"I never planned to have a party, but by Sunday night I had a house full of people!"

"My nephew said he had a great time. It sounded like Bree did too." She took another bite.

"Remember when I told you about the one piece of evidence that was found? A white button?"

"Sure. What about it?"

"It looks like it might be Breana's button, but, of course, she can't be the murderer...."

"Of course not!" Julia laughed. "That's a ridiculous idea."

Ridiculous or not, I couldn't shake it. In my mind, I pictured sweet little Breana sneaking up on Henry with a loaded gun. But my imagination would not go so far as to have Bree pull the trigger.

I finished painting the fourth cowboy, adding whiskers, a holster and gun. Shortly before five, I packed up my paints and carried them to the truck.

"Hi, Jo!" Breana said, circling her car and heading into the Crazy Horse.

"How were your classes?" I asked.

She stopped next to my truck. "Lovely classes, they are. Is something wrong, Josephine?"

"No, nothing, I left your clothes with Alonzo. Did you know that your blouse is missing a button?"

"Oh, my, yes! The button was missin' when Lois gave it to me, it was. I planned to sew one on, if only time wasn't so precious, would you believe that? And since it was the bottom button, it didn't matter so much. I'll be off now," she laughed and walked into the saloon.

I ran after her into the building. "Bree, I have a question...."

She spun around to face me. "Indeed, Josephine, what's on your mind?"

"When did Lois give you the blouse?"

"Huh? Well, let me think. The day before they went on holiday, I believe it was." She looked at me like I'd gone mad.

I thanked her, drove straight to Watsonville and parked my truck in front of Alicia's house. I knocked on the door and Trigger let me in. No matter what was going on in my life, Trigger hugs always helped.

"Jo, this is a happy surprise!" Alicia said, giving me a big hug.

"I need to talk to you, Allie. I have new information in the Hobblestone case, and I want to see what you think." I followed her to the kitchen table and a cup of hot tea. I told her how I'd put the police onto Rotsider's trail and laid out the evidence, including the Minerant.

Alicia took a sip of tea. "Sounds like a pretty good case against him, Jo, for robbery. But why would he kill Henry for the ring if the stone had already been replaced with glass?"

"You're right, Allie. I think I was wrong about Rotsider. But here's a new scenario. A button was found at the scene of the murder, and I think it came from Lois' blouse that she later gave to Breana."

"That's it?" Alicia rolled her eyes up to the ceiling.

"That's not all. Lois just happens to be in Antwerp as we speak. Maybe Henrietta discovered her sapphire had been replaced with blue glass and Lois had to kill her to keep her quiet. The ring was proof of what Lois had done so she hid it in a sack of oats, unless Henrietta hid it in the oats before she was murdered. Either way, the ring is proof of a swindle."

"What are you going to do, Jo?"

"I'll have to notify the Sheriff again. Actually, I'm a little worried about Tom. I can't imagine him being involved in this. Lois said he's been sick the whole trip. When she told me she was catching a train to Antwerp, she didn't even mention Tom." Suddenly, I had a rush of cold prickles all over my body.

Alicia handed me the phone.

"Thanks, Allie." I dialed, got Officer Sayer on the line, and arranged a meeting at the Trippys' house for eight-thirty. Maybe by then I'd have all the loose ends accounted for, like who searched the Trippy house and Henry's house. I was pretty sure the brothers did it—with Elvira's blessing.

Alicia talked me into staying for dinner—not surprising. Trigger's homemade chicken enchiladas smelled so good. There was no way I could not stay. Besides, Trigger was proud to have me try his cooking. Ernie made the rice and refried beans, and I made the salad while Alicia took Tansey for a walk in the neighborhood. I heard the front door close and Alicia and Tansey entered the kitchen.

"Jo, come here a minute." She pulled me over to the dining room window. "Same red truck?"

"Yep, same idiots! The lawnmower in the back is a dead giveaway!" I'd have to have a talk with Elvira.

We finished eating dinner around seven-thirty. I apologized for my quick exit, explaining that the Sheriff's deputies would be waiting for me in Prunedale.

The brothers followed me all the way to Langley Gulch Road, and mindlessly stayed with me as I turned up Henry's driveway.

I stopped in front of the shingled house and honked the horn.

Elvira flung the door open and planted herself on the porch, hands on hips.

I rolled down my window and thumbed at the Chevy truck behind me.

"Tell your friends the party's over!" I shouted. I cranked the wheel, careened around the eucalyptus, spraying gravel on the Chevy as I left the property.

I parked in the Trippy garage and barely had time to feed all the animals before the doorbell rang.

I opened the door and my jaw dropped.

"Ms. Stuart, I'm Agent Ingram. May I come in?" He held a badge for me to look at.

"Ah, sure, Mr. Agent, please come in," I muttered. The man was young, fit and dressed in a really nice black suit. He sat down on one sofa. I sat on the wingback chair.

"Ms. Stuart, the County Sheriff's Department has been in contact with my people. We've been working with Interpol in Belgium to find and capture Mr. Rotsider...."

"Oh, but it's not Rotsider who murdered Henry. It was Lois Trippy."

Agent Ingram cocked his head. "And you have evidence to support this claim?"

"I do. I mean, I did, but I gave everything to Officers Lund and Sayer. And they have the button that was found at the murder scene, the one that actually fell off Lois' blouse. "By the way, Lois is in Antwerp right now, at the Minerant."

"How do you know that Ms. Trippy is in Antwerp?" he asked.

"I talked to Lois on the phone this morning and she said she was about to board a train to Antwerp. I didn't put two and two together until Breana told me that it was Lois' blouse she was wearing that lost a button. It all makes perfect sense...."

"Can you tell me where Mrs. Trippy is staying?" He stopped writing in his notepad, letting his blue-eyed lock onto me. There was a sense of urgency in his eyes and his voice. I wondered if he knew more than what I was telling him.

"I've told you everything I know," I said.

"Here's my card. Call me if you come across anything new. We appreciate your help, Ms. Stuart." He stood and walked to the door.

"What's going to happen next?"

He stopped and turned around to listen to me as I spoke:

"Will the FBI catch Lois? And did I tell you I'm worried about her husband?"

"No, you didn't mention a husband."

"Well, Tom's a nice guy. Lois said he's been sick for the whole trip—that's fifteen days so far, and now I think maybe she's ditched him."

"We'll check into the situation," he assured me. Ingram shook my hand and walked outside to his black SUV.

I closed the front door and tried not to think about poor old Tom and his nutty wife. I went to the den, curled up on a plaid loveseat with Solow at my feet, turned on the TV and fell asleep. I dreamt I was eating chicken enchiladas swimming in apple cider vinegar and marshmallows.

I woke up with a stomachache and decided to trundle off to bed.

I stood up.

Solow howled.

The doorbell rang.

Moving in a sleepy fog, I felt my way down the dark hall and crept across the living room to the front door, Solow at my heels. I flipped on the porch light and peeked out the peephole. Two men stood waiting.

Solow growled.

I opened the door and Tom Trippy stumbled into the house with help from a cab driver. He dropped into the first mauve sofa he came to. Breathing hard, he looked up at me with bloodshot eyes, his unshaven jaw twisted into a grimace. He handed the cab driver a wad of cash.

"The man needs medical attention," the driver said to me, and walked out the door to his cab.

"Tom, what happened to you?"

"Just need a little rest. Help me to my bed, would ya?" Tom tried to stand up so I grabbed his arm and pulled. He was finally standing but shaky. With lots of effort, we zigzagged our way down the hall. I was able to help him to his bed and hoist him in, shoes and all. As soon as Tom was settled in, I called David. The phone rang several times. He answered in a slow husky voice.

"Josie, it's four in the morning...."

"I know what time it is—actually I didn't—but now that you mention it...never mind, this is important. Tom's home and he looks awful. A cab driver dropped him off...."

"You're kidding! They're not supposed to be home for two more weeks." David sounded wide-awake.

"I would have asked a few questions but he's exhausted. He's in bed now...."

"I'll be right over." We hung up.

I checked on Tom. He hadn't moved, but I could hear him breathing. I pulled his shoes off and covered him with a quilt. He looked ten years older than the day he and his wife had left Prunedale to go to Europe.

Twenty minutes later, David burst through the front door. "Josie, where is he?"

I pointed to the hall. "Second bedroom on the right."

David gave me a peck on the cheek and hurried down the hall to find his old friend and former boss.

A minute later, I joined them.

In the light from one small reading lamp, David bent over Tom and laid a hand on his pale forehead, obviously checking for fever. Tom hadn't moved an inch since I'd heaved his limp legs up onto the bed. David found his friend's left wrist and held it until he was sure there was a pulse.

"Not very strong."

"What should we do?" I asked, feeling panic overtaking good judgment.

"We'll wait till he wakes up, ask him a few questions and then decide what to do." David's voice was calm. I trusted his constraint.

My first inclination was to run hysterically in circles, call an ambulance, the Mounted Police and the Coast Guard. Fortunately, David was my anchor. I listened to him and agreed we should wait till morning, and let the poor man rest.

David turned off the lamp and we quietly tiptoed through the house to the kitchen for a light snack. I flipped the light switch.

"What in Sam Hill?"

David laughed nervously at the cockatoo's comment. "He really belts it out, that ol' bird."

"I'm used to him. I just give him a cracker now and then with a cup of tea…."

"Tea? You give the bird tea?"

"Chamomile tea to calm him down," I said as I put the teakettle on the stove. "I have some potato salad…."

"I'm not really hungry." He poked his head into the fridge. "But that fried chicken looks good."

We sat at the kitchen table talking and snacking until the sun came up. I let Solow out the back door and marveled at the beautiful sunrise. Early morning was not my time of day but it was a pretty sight, all quiet and dewy until Roscoe began Wednesday's cock-a-doodle-doo solo.

I stepped back into the kitchen in time to see Tom lumber into the room. He plopped into a chair and sighed. His sunken eyes blinked as morning sun streaked through the windows.

"Cup of coffee, Tom?" David asked. Tom nodded and David put Mr. Coffee to work.

"Are you hungry?" I asked.

Tom shook his head. I noticed dark circles under gray eyes with no light in them.

"That's okay, old boy. We have all day to relax," David said, patting Tom gently on his back. "Anything you want to tell us about the trip?"

Tom stared blankly at Boris. "Who's he?"

"This is Boris," I said, "from Henry's?"

"Oh." But he obviously didn't understand. I wondered if his mind would return in time.

"Boris wants a cracker."

I found a cracker for the mouthy bird. He seemed to be satisfied for the moment. Now that Tom was home, I wondered if I should pack my things and move back to Aromas at the end of the day.

David made a nice breakfast for the three of us.

Tom ate slowly, quietly.

Maybe after work I'd learn more about Tom's traumatic experience.

I was sure David could pull the truth out of him, man-to-man.

Chapter Nineteen

Wednesday morning I left David and Tom in Prunedale, checked in at the Crazy Horse, set up my paints and ladder and began painting a dance hall girl. Somehow I already had a picture of her in my head. I knew she had dark eyes and black hair and her skin was milky white. She wore a long red off-the-shoulder dress with white apple blossoms pinned to her hair. There were several silver bracelets on one wrist and a string of black pearls around her neck.

As I painted, a cold draft touched the back of my neck. I heard a soft clucking noise and turned to see who was there. I was alone except for Alonzo who was walking my way. He stared at the rough beginning of the dance hall girl.

"I can already see who she is," he said. "The eyes, the tilt of her head...I've seen her before."

Two couples entered the room and ordered lunch. Alonzo waited on them but kept an eye on the painting, coming back to it, over and over again.

As I painted, my mind wandered off to Europe. What was it like to be in Antwerp with a couple of million dollars to spend? Lois and Mr. Rotsider in Antwerp at the same time was the biggest coincidence I could imagine. My daydreams continued until Julia walked into the restaurant at two o'clock.

All of a sudden, I was hungry.

"Josephine, the lady you're painting, do you know her?" she asked.

"No, but I can see her in my head. Wow, she's practically done. I might be able to finish her today." I'd made more progress than expected. It had been so easy.

Alonzo remarked again how familiar the lady in the painting looked. He asked if we'd like to try his new house special, free of charge.

Free had my vote.

Julia wasn't sure she'd like sea bass, but said she'd try it if it came with a glass of wine.

Alonzo laughed and agreed.

Julia and I talked about the latest news about Belgium, and Tom's unexpected arrival. Julia lamented the fact that she'd probably never see a paycheck for her work at the Jewelry Company.

Alonzo arrived at our table with two platters of fish and all the trimmings. He poured three glasses of wine and sat down beside his *Tia Julianna* for a few minutes of socializing.

Julia was impressed with her nephew's cooking, telling me that we ought to eat at the Crazy Horse more often. I only had about four more hours of painting until I was finished, but I told her we'd have to get together for lunch in the future. San Juan Bautista wasn't too far to go to meet a friend.

When our lunch plates were empty and our tummies full, Julia suddenly gasped. "Josephine, I forgot to give you this! I was going to tell you before lunch, then the food came and I forgot all about it...." She pulled a piece of folded notepaper from her pocket and handed it to me. "I was cleaning behind Mr. Rotsider's desk, and there it was."

I unfolded the paper and read the note aloud.

"Meet me at the Minerant main entrance, noon, Thursday, September 23rd.

Love and kisses, Lois."

"Oh, my God! He's going to meet her!" I smacked the table with the palm of my hand.

"I was afraid of that," Julia moaned. "There goes my career and Mom's necklace."

"Julia, I need to call Agent Ingram right away." I grabbed my purse, thanked Julia and Alonzo and dashed out. From the cab of my truck, I called the agent's number. As soon as he agreed to meet me at the Trippy house, I peeled out from the curb and roared through San Juan Bautista. My mind was full of Lois and Sam and poor old Tom as I stormed across the mid-afternoon landscape toward Prunedale. I cut the engine in front of the Trippy house.

A shiny black SUV cooled its wheels in the Trippy driveway.

I rushed into the house barely able to catch my breath.

Tom, obviously showered and shaved, sat in a white wingback chair looking healthy, but lost.

David sat on one sofa and Agent Ingram sat on the other.

I squeezed in beside David.

"Ms. Stuart, you have news for me?" Ingram asked.

"Yes, I have something you need to see." I handed the note to David first for a quick read, then passed it on to Ingram. I turned back to David and whispered in his ear.

David stood and asked Tom to go with him to the backyard.

Tom stood up and dutifully followed David out of the room.

"Where did this come from, and who found it?" the agent asked.

I waited a moment for Tom to leave the room with David.

"My friend, Julia, found the note behind a desk when she was cleaning the jewelry shop floor. She knows all about the Minerant and stuff like that so she knew what this note was all about."

"If that's all you have for me, I'll be going." Agent Ingram stood up to go.

I stood up. "Will the FBI be looking for Lois and Mr. Rotsider?"

"Everything is in place, but we'll forward this new information right away. This will help us a great deal, knowing the exact time and place of their meeting. It won't be long now. I'll let you know how it turns out," he said. "Thank you, Ms. Stuart." He turned and walked to his vehicle.

I moseyed into the house, feeling sad for Tom but glad that law enforcement was going to take care of everything in Antwerp. I wandered through the house, wondering if I'd miss living on white carpet; but when I thought about my own house, I could hardly wait to be back there.

I found David in the backyard, playing ball with the four-legged boys.

"Where's Tom?"

"He wanted to go back to bed."

"So what exactly is wrong with Tom? Did you take him to a doctor?"

"He's a broken man. His wife poisoned him and now it looks like she's running off with the jeweler. I did take him to see his doctor today."

"And?"

"Doc said it will take some time for the meds to get out of his system, but Tom *will* be all right. When I think about his marriage, it was a mismatch at best. Lois was younger and pretty. Tom had a great career; but now he just wants companionship—a good wife." David put his hand on mine. "I always thought Lois wasn't very smart—you know, the way she just giggled all the time. Well, she sure out-smarted all of us. Poor Tom!" His voice faded to almost nothing.

David and I sat shoulder to shoulder on the lawn swing, contemplating Tom's situation. The boys were passed out on the lawn. We watched the ripples on the water and a hummingbird that thought he might like a drink. I could have stayed there all day except that I had a painting to finish and all my painting equipment was still in the restaurant.

David asked me to stay, but he knew I had to go so he walked me to my truck and kissed me goodbye. Energized by his kiss, I poured myself into finishing the *Lady in the Red Dress*. My mind had been so full of Henry's murder and the Minerant that I hardly remembered painting the woman. I finished her at six o'clock. Alonzo let me stay and finish the painting because he was fascinated. He kept saying he knew her. I didn't think much about it until Daisy checked in for the evening shift and gawked at the painting.

"Josephine, looks like you *have* seen her," she said.

A chill whipped around my neck, causing me to shudder. I didn't see anyone, but I smelled apple blossoms, like the ones I'd painted on the long black hair of the lady in red.

Breana joined the critique. "Now that's a proper day's work if ever I saw one. Our Lady in Red is well represented, indeed." She helped me by carrying a ladder to the truck. We came back for a second load, Alonzo paid me, and Breana walked with me outside. She held out her left hand.

"Bree, is that diamond real?"

"Mother of God, it better be. It comes from dear Alonzo, the love of me life, he is," she beamed.

I hugged her and wished her nothing but happiness.

She waved goodbye as I began my drive to Prunedale for the second time that day. I felt happy for Breana and sad for Tom. It occurred to me that He gives us so much and sometimes He takes it away, but the sun comes up right on time through it all.

I parked in the Trippy garage and found David sitting at the kitchen table reading the paper.

"Where's Tom?"

"He was up for awhile and then went back to bed. Tom and I had a long talk while you were at work. He told me that he and Lois had been asked by Henrietta to witness her will. Stilts read it out loud and then he and Lois signed it."

"That's funny. Lois told me she didn't know if there *was* a will. So that's how she knew about the ring," I said. "That's how she knew it was worth a fortune and how she knew who'd inherit it. Did Tom tell you who gets the ring?"

"Elvira."

"Who gets the house?"

"Breana," he smiled.

"I wish I could tell her right now. That's so wonderful!" I said as a couple of happy tears rolled down my cheeks.

David kissed them away.

I looked up at Tom standing in the doorway.

"Sorry, I just needed a glass of water," he said, and helped himself to a bottle from the fridge.

The doorbell rang. I opened the door and was handed a shallow box full of many little boxes of Chinese food. David paid the delivery boy, and we devoured most of the food. Even Tom did his share. He was coming back to life.

During dinner, David told me his plan for the next few days. I would go home tomorrow, he would stay with Tom for a couple of days, and I would check in on his kittens occasionally. A few kittens sounded a lot easier than the crazy animal house I'd lived in for the last three weeks.

Thursday, we followed the plan. I packed up and drove home with Solow. David stayed with Tom. I'd just arrived at my home in Aromas when my cell phone rang. It was David.

"Josie, I got a call from Agent Ingram…."

"What did he say?" I asked, barely able to spit out the words, I was so excited.

"They caught Lois and Sam at the main entrance to the Minerant exactly at noon. Ingram wanted to thank you over the phone. He said the sapphire is safe and will be used as evidence. I guess Elvira will have to wait a little longer for her fortune."

"That's good, I'm glad it's over," I said, feeling the pinch in my neck loosen. "I had a call from Breana yesterday. She said Mr. Forman asked her to attend the reading of the will next week. She sounded very excited. I didn't tell her she's going to get Henry's house. She'll be so happy!"

"Speaking of happy, I'll be happy when we get back to a normal life where you live next door and I can come over to see you when I want. Take good care of my kittens. I'll be home soon."

Epilogue

Breana and Alonzo eloped to Tahoe, taking Aunt Julia with them to witness the happy occasion. The Crazy Horse Saloon was closed for three days. When the newlyweds attended the reading of the will, they were shocked and surprised to learn that they'd inherited Henry's place. They started off their family farm by adopting Boris, Willy and Roscoe with Tom's blessing.

Tom recovered his health and lost his depression, thanks to David, golf and a new lady friend. He had not seen Lois since their trip to Europe, except for an unflattering picture of his wife on the front page of the *Sentinel,* handcuffed and wearing unattractive orange overalls.

Mr. Rotsider was not charged with any crimes because stupid isn't necessarily a crime. He'd exchanged glass for sapphire under Lois' direction. She'd asked him to meet her at the Minerant. Sam knew she wanted to sell the stone so he went all the way to Antwerp to dissuade her, he claimed.

Elvira and Nate drove back to their home in Texas, knowing they'd eventually be millionaires, once the prosecution was through with the ring.

Allen and Marvin started their own detective agency. They were *up-for-hire* with plenty of diverse experience behind them. Elvira had hired them to bug Lois' phone and Lois had hired them to mow the yard, clean her house and search the two houses for the ring while spying on Josephine. Allen confessed to swiping the sugar bowl but no charges were made. The brothers kept their Ace Brothers lawn mowing and handyman business, just in case.

THE END

ABOUT THE AUTHOR

 Author Joyce Oroz takes her past experiences as a mural artist and tucks them neatly into her stories as needed. Real life for Oroz these days consists of adventures with the grandchildren, large gatherings with family and friends and the day-to-day reading, writing, painting, walking the dog and battling invading packs of gophers. She loves her husband, dog and California routine. Writing is the sweet topping on her busy life.

Other books by Joyce Oroz:

- *Secure the Ranch*
- *Read My Lipstick*
- *Shaking in Her Flip Flops*
- *Beetles in the Boxcar*
- *Cuckoo Clock Caper*
- *Roller Rubout*